TAKE WH

Sophie was only a teenager, but she
knew she would never love, had never
loved, anyone but her stepbrother
Robert. But her whole family, including Robert, disapproved, and hoped
she would get over the feeling. Were
they right—or was Sophie?

TAKE WHAT YOU WANT

BY

ANNE MATHER

MILLS & BOON LIMITED
17–19 FOLEY STREET
LONDON W1A 1DR

First published 1975
This edition 1975

© Anne Mather 1975

ISBN 0 263 71858 1

Made and printed in Great Britain by
Richard Clay (The Chaucer Press) Ltd, Bungay, Suffolk

'Take what you want,' said God.
'Take it—and pay for it.'

OLD SPANISH PROVERB

CHAPTER ONE

SOPHIE shifted her weight from one foot to the other, aware that her every move was being monitored by the two soldiers squatting on their suitcases a few feet away. The train was crowded with holidaymakers, and not having had the opportunity to book a seat, Sophie had had to spend the journey jammed up against her cases in the no-man's-land area between two of the compartments. Not that she had minded. She was too excited at the prospect of going home to care to spend several hours sitting absolutely still, and although two men had offered her their seats she had politely declined. Still, their gesture confirmed her growing maturity, she reflected, and even in the bottle-green skirt and matching school blazer, she looked like a young woman. She had been aware for some time now that men found her physically attractive, and although she had always enjoyed the knowledge she was only now beginning to appreciate its advantages.

A young woman carrying a baby passed on her way to the toilet compartment and Sophie squeezed her slender body further into her corner, refusing to acknowledge the sympathetic smiles of the soldiers. One of them had already offered her a cigarette which she had refused, and while she accepted that they were harmless enough she wanted no complications to interrupt her daydreams of her reunion with Robert.

It was eighteen months since she had seen Robert, eighteen months since he had held her and kissed her and shaken her small world to its core...

But he was to be home these holidays. Her father

had written and told her so. Of course, Simon would be there, too, and in spite of her preference for her older stepbrother, she had always found Simon an easier conquest, and consequently had used him shamelessly.

Robert was different. Robert was unpredictable. But with Robert she shared an affinity. Robert—who had taught her to ride and swim and play tennis, who had talked to her as an equal about his plans and ambitions, who had first interested her in books and music and poetry.

She peered out at the green countryside flashing by the windows of the train. She could remember clearly the first time she had seen Robert. Her mother had died when she was born and her father, a busy London doctor, had employed a series of housekeepers to look after them. But it hadn't worked. He had had too little time to spend with his small daughter and realising that without a mother either the child was being neglected, he had thrown up his London practice and moved to Conwynneth, a village not far from Hereford on the Welsh borders. Here life moved at a much more leisurely pace and Doctor Kemble relaxed and felt young again and involved himself and his small daughter in the social life of the community.

Laura Ydris was a widow with two sons. She ran the small inn in the village single-handed since her husband had been killed two years previously in a road accident. Her younger son, Simon, was twelve, while the elder boy, Robert, was sixteen. Both boys attended the grammar school in Hereford.

Sophie's father began spending a lot of time at the inn, and it was no real surprise to anybody when he and Laura decided to get married. Sophie had been four at that time, round and plump and inclined to be shy of strangers, her short fair hair framing chubby

8

features.

From the very beginning, Sophie had taken to her stepmother. Laura was nothing like the wicked stepmothers redolent of fairy tales. She was small, too, dark and vivacious, and she won Sophie's heart completely when she confided that she had always wanted a little girl of her own to care for.

The problems, were there to have been any, might have occurred with the two boys. But both Robert and Simon had realised that their mother was finding it very hard keeping the inn going alone, and they were glad she was going to be able to give up working and have a real home again. Besides, they liked Doctor Kemble and were old enough to appreciate their parents' mutual needs. Sophie had been in her element having two older brothers suddenly provided for her. They had spoilt her, she realised that now, but at the time she had seen nothing selfish in demanding their undivided attention.

Sophie had met Simon first. Robert was away in Switzerland on a school holiday when the engagement was first announced, and by the time he came home Sophie and Simon were quite good friends. It was a novelty for the boys to have a sister, too, but from the minute Sophie encountered her elder stepbrother's steady gaze she had become his devoted admirer. He was a popular boy, usually in the company of a crowd of young people, but he was never too busy to talk to Sophie. And girl-friends, in particular, grew impatient at having to compete with a child!

In two years, Robert went away to university, and the rambling old house which Doctor Kemble had bought at the time of his second marriage had suddenly seemed terribly quiet. For four years Sophie had had to accept that she only saw Robert in the holidays, but when he graduated he came back to Conwynneth to work for an engineering firm in Hereford.

By this time Simon was starting at university, but Sophie didn't miss Simon half so much. Besides, she had Robert back again, and at twelve years old Sophie found her mature stepbrother absolutely fascinating. She was just becoming aware of herself as a female creature and she didn't altogether understand why she felt curious pains in her stomach whenever Robert looked at her in a certain way or why, when he went out with girls, she felt sick and restless.

She was utterly shattered therefore when her father suddenly announced that she was to be sent away to boarding school. She didn't want to go to boarding school. That would mean only seeing Robert in the holidays again, and she was mature enough to realise that he could conceivably get married while she was at school.

But for once her father and stepmother were immune from her desperate appeals, and even Robert seemed cool and aloof, unwilling to offer her his support. She had to go, and for the first term she spent every night in tears, impervious to the sympathy offered her by would-be confidantes.

Gradually, though, she began to realise that crying was not going to get her anywhere. Her most sensible plan would be to work especially hard, pass every examination in sight and get back to Conwynneth as soon as she possibly could.

But while she worked her way through school, word reached her that Robert's career was expanding. He was an intelligent man and he had been offered a better position with a London-based firm of constructional engineers with world-wide connections. He leased an apartment in London and then went on his first overseas assignment to Central Africa. It meant that when Sophie went home for two lots of holidays she didn't see him at all, and she spent the time mooching about the house, refusing even to join Simon and his friends on a camping expedition to the Lake District. She knew that her parents were concerned about her, but hoped they didn't know what was depressing her.

She took her Ordinary Level examinations at fifteen and succeeded in getting eleven passes, much to the delight and admiration of her family and her teachers. The Christmas holidays that followed, Robert was home again and joining his family for the festivities, and his congratulations meant more to her than anyone else's had done. And it was during those holidays that Robert had kissed her . . .

Her fingers curled into her palms. The Kembles had had guests for Christmas, friends of her father's from London, two couples and their five children. She suspected her father had invited them deliberately in an effort to arouse her from the apathy she had shown in the summer vacation. But with Robert staying in the house, Sophie was far from apathetic.

The other teenagers, a girl of sixteen and four boys whose ages ranged from thirteen to eighteen, were all right, but so far as Sophie was concerned they were pretty callow compared to her handsome stepbrothers. Even Simon, who at twenty-three was now teaching at the junior school in Conwynneth, was a more interesting proposition. Sophie had been brought up with adults and consequently her tastes were more mature. She enjoyed pop music, of course, and talking about current teenage idols, but thanks to Robert she was equally at home with Mahler and Isaac Stern.

Over the festive occasion, she joined in all the fun and games instituted in the main for the younger people's benefit, but all the while she was intensely conscious of Robert in the background—and the girl he had brought with him from London. She was a secretary, so her stepmother had told her, working in the London office of the company which employed Robert; but Sophie didn't like her.

Not that she had any concrete reasons for not doing so. None she could put her finger on, that was. On the contrary, Emma, as the girl was called, was pretty and friendly, no different from a dozen other girls Robert had brought to Penn Warren during the years of Sophie's adolescence.

But there was something about the way she looked at Robert that troubled Sophie. At times she caught Emma watching him with a purely speculative gleam in her eyes, and she had the distinct suspicion that Emma would not be so easy to shake off. And then something happened which drove all other considerations out of her mind ...

On Christmas Eve and Christmas Day the Kembles and their guests had enjoyed the family festivities, but on Boxing Night they always had a party. Several people from the village were invited including the local vet and his wife, some farmers and their wives, and even the vicar put in an appearance. There was lots to eat and drink and the long buffet tables which Laura and Mrs. Forrest, her daily, had arranged groaned beneath the weight of cold chickens and turkey, ham and tongue, pies and pastries of all kinds. An enormous dish of trifle was flanked by an equally enormous plum pudding, and there was wine and punch as well as all kinds of spirits.

Sophie wore the dress her parents had given her for Christmas. It was her first long dress, apart from a couple of hostess gowns she had used for parties at school, and as it was made of honey-brown velvet it gave her a golden look. A holiday in Spain with her parents three months ago had left a golden tan on her skin and as she wore little make-up apart from eye-shadow and an apricot lip-salve her whole appearance toned with the dress. Her hair was long now, but as straight as ever, which fortunately was fashionable. When she surveyed herself in her mirror before going downstairs she knew she looked adult, and the look in Robert's eyes when he had first seen her had sent the blood rushing madly through her veins. Then he had assumed his usual affectionate tolerance towards her and told her she would have all the boys chasing her. It was not what she had wanted to hear, but Emma's quickly disguised envy had made up in some strange way for her stepbrother's apparent indifference.

From time to time during the course of the evening, she had thought she felt Robert's eyes upon her, but every time she turned to look at him he was talking to someone else. He didn't even ask her for a dance, and she hid her disappointment as she had always done by teasing Simon. Not that Simon seemed to mind. On the contrary, when he held her close on the dance floor Sophie sensed that he was not just pretending to enjoy it. His behaviour obviously piqued the other girls there, older girls like Vicky Page, the vet's daughter, who was attracted by both the doctor's stepsons.

It was quite late when Sophie realised that Robert had disappeared, and her heart pounded as she looked round for Emma. But Emma was still there, dancing with Harold Venables, a farmer from Apsdale, and she breathed a sigh of relief.

As though her stepmother had just become aware that Robert was missing, too, Laura approached her and Simon at that moment and said: 'Simon, be a darling and dance with Vicky, won't you? She's been looking at you with cow's eyes for the last hour and a half. And you, Sophie—go and find Robert! He's probably in your father's study. You know how he gets bored at these affairs.'

So Sophie had left the party and gone along the hall to her father's study, and sure enough, Robert was there, stretched out in her father's chair, his feet resting lazily on the desk, reading a manual on structural engineering. He looked up when she entered the room and his eyes were wary.

'Your mother sent me to find you,' Sophie had said, feeling rather like an intruder.

Robert did not bother to get up but sat there regarding her with steady grey eyes. 'Did she?'

'Yes.' Sophie had hovered uncertainly by the door. 'Are you coming back to join the rest of us?'

'I don't think so, thanks.'

He had returned his attentions to the book as though that was the end of the matter, and Sophie had been annoyed. He had dismissed her without even a word of apology.

With a determined set to her mouth she had entered the study and closed the door and walked round the desk to where he was stretched out. When he eventually became aware of her standing there in front of him, he had looked up again and said resignedly: 'Run away and enjoy yourself, Sophie. I'm perfectly happy here. I've no intention of getting myself plastered when I have to drive back to London in the morning.'

Sophie had stared at him angrily, upset at the realisation that he would be leaving in a few hours and it might be months before she saw him again. 'Don't you think you're being rather boorish?' she had demanded. 'Sitting here alone like some temperamental prima donna!'

Robert had smiled at this, a lazy mocking smile that did nothing for her temper. Controlling a desire to slap his lean intelligent face, she had said: 'You

14

haven't even danced with me!'

Robert's eyes had flickered then. 'You have boys of your own age to dance with,' he pointed out. 'And besides, Simon is more than eager to accommodate you.'

Sophie had really lost her temper then and she had snatched the book from him and thrown it aside, grasping his hands and trying to pull him up out of the chair. But he had resisted, dragging her down instead, down on to his knee, on to the hard muscles of his thighs, and he had kissed her in an urgent adult way that had sent the blood flaming along her veins and her senses spinning. Under that passionate assault her lips had parted and her fingers had slid up to his neck where the thick dark hair brushed his collar. When he had finally let her go, her legs had been like jelly and his face had been pale and shaken. He had muttered a rough apology and left her, and she had known then that things between them could never be the same again.

She had not seen Robert again before he left for London. The following morning she had intended to be up early, but exhaustion after the strenuous evening had taken its toll and by the time she came downstairs both Robert and Emma had gone.

Her faint hopes that she might see him before returning to boarding school were dashed by a telephone call to her stepmother informing them that Robert was leaving for the Far East at the end of the week, and she had returned to school feeling more depressed than before.

But all that had been eighteen months ago now. During that time Sophie had matured considerably, and although the holidays she had spent with her parents had been at times when Robert was away on some job or other, she had consoled herself with the thought

15

that he was giving her time to grow up before involving himself more deeply. After all, she had had the sense to realise that their parents would never have countenanced any kind of a relationship between them while she was still at school. But now her schooldays were over. She had six months to decide whether or not to apply for university entrance next year, and during those six months . . .

She sighed, raising her shoulders in a little self-satisfied gesture before letting them fall again. A lot could happen in six months and in less than an hour she would see Robert again.

She turned back from the window and encountered the admiring gaze of one of the soldiers. The message in his eyes was unmistakable and it gave her a warm feeling inside to know that she was attractive. Surely Robert must see the difference in her, the way her breasts had swelled, the narrowness of her waist, the provocative curve of her hips. Laura had promised these holidays that she would buy her a whole new wardrobe suitable to a young woman who had successfully gained three 'A' levels and who was leaving the school portals for good. She intended to buy some long feminine clothes, skirts and dresses and trouser suits, that accentuated her femininity rather than detracted from it.

She looked out of the window again and her stomach plunged. The tracks were widening out into shunting yards, they passed a signal box that indicated that Hereford station was not too far distant. Glory, they were almost there!

She looked down at her feet. Her two cases stood side by side along with the school briefcase which contained all her books. She had had quite a struggle along Paddington station until a friendly porter, busy with the pigskin luggage of a rather haughty-looking

16

middle-aged woman, had taken pity on her and hefted her cases on to his trolley and deposited them by the open door of the second class compartment for no charge, much to his employer's annoyance.

'Can I give you a hand?'

It was one of the soldiers. They were running into Hereford station now and Sophie's attention was diverted from scanning the platform with heightening excitement.

'What—oh, well, I'm sure I can manage,' she demurred, half impatiently, but the young man was persistent.

'It's no trouble,' he insisted, shaking his head. 'We all get out here. Is someone meeting you?'

Sophie cast a hasty look at the barrier as the train slowed. 'I should think so.'

The soldier grinned, 'We should be so lucky!'

She smiled at this, and then with a lurch the train ground to a halt and she rolled down the window and lent out to open the door.

They were among the first to emerge into the humid, diesel-clogged air of late afternoon. The two soldiers had taken charge of a suitcase each and Sophie was left with only her briefcase to carry. Their attentions had distracted her and she was fumbling for her ticket when a cool, masculine voice said: 'Hello, Sophie. It's good to see you again.'

Sophie looked up, her colour rising, her hands beginning to tremble uncontrollably. She hadn't see his approach and she felt a ridiculous sense of resentment towards the two soldiers who had deprived her of that. But he hadn't changed—at least, not a lot. He was perhaps a little leaner than she remembered, and had his grey eyes always had that steel edge to them? His tanned features bore witness to the months he had spent in warmer climes, and his hair was thicker and fell in a heavy swathe across his forehead. Heavy-lidded eyes, narrow cheekbones, a mouth that right now looked thin and uncompromising. And tall—dwarfing even her five feet six inches. He was wearing tight-fitting jeans and an open-necked denim shirt and he exuded an aura of strength and disturbing masculinity. And yet for all that, she sensed that he was suppressing anger. But why? Did he imagine she had picked up the two soldiers who were now exchanging glances and clearly wishing they had not offered their services?

Sophie made a helpless little movement of her shoulders. This was not how she had planned their reunion to be. She had waited over a year for this. She would not allow anyone to spoil it.

With a determination born of desperation she dropped her briefcase and ignoring everyone but Robert, she stepped close to him and threw her arms round his neck, pressing her lips to his mouth. Because of the unexpectedness of her action, Robert's hands came up automatically to close around her forearms to prevent them from overbalancing, but within seconds their pressure had hardened and he was thrusting her roughly away from him.

'*Sophie!*' he muttered angrily, and the two soldiers set down her cases and with embarrassed smiles walked on. 'Sophie, for God's sake!' He raked a hand through his hair and cast a swift look around them to assure himself that they were not under observation.

Sophie was unrepentant. In spite of his anger, just for a moment Robert's mouth had responded to hers, and it was sufficient to convince her that he was not indifferent to her. So she smiled, a lovely, confident smile that widened her mouth and filled her green eyes with tawny lights. 'What did you expect?' she asked mockingly. 'That we should shake hands?'

Robert looked down at her impatiently. 'Is this all your luggage?'

Sophie glanced round. 'Mmm.' Then she looked up at him again. 'Aren't you glad to see me, Robert?'

He made an irritated gesture. 'Of course I'm glad to see you, Sophie. I already said so.' He picked up the two cases. 'Can you manage the briefcase?'

Sophie sighed and obediently picked it up. 'Yes, I can manage, thank you.'

Robert cast another unsmiling look in her direction and then strode away down the platform so that she had, perforce, to hurry to keep up with him. Once through the barrier, he led the way outside and halted beside a steel grey sports saloon parked in the yard. It was even more humid outside beneath the lowering clouds that were threatening rain, but to Sophie it was heaven to be back home again.

She spread her arms extravagantly and then concentrated her attention on the vehicle. 'This is new, isn't it?' she commented admiringly. 'What is it? An Aston Martin?'

'No. A Jensen,' stated Robert flatly, stowing her cases in the boot. 'Get in. It's not locked.'

Shrugging, Sophie opened the long door and climbed into the low passenger seat with its curved back and headrest. The instrument panel fascinated her and she was examining the various controls when Robert opened his door and levered his length in beside her. Immediately all else lost significance and she wondered what he would do if she attempted to kiss him again. It was a tantalising proposition and she turned sideways in her seat to look at him.

'You'd better fasten the safety strap,' he observed curtly, apparently unmoved by her scrutiny, and with an exclamation she swung round and did as she was told. She quelled the urge to make some insolent retort and looking at him out of the corners of her eyes, she said:

'This is a super car, isn't it? I wish I could drive.'

'I expect your father will arrange for you to take lessons now that you've finished school,' he remarked coolly, inserting the ignition key and starting the powerful engine. He opened his window and looked out, reversing expertly out of the parking space. 'Congratulations, by the way. I hear you did well in your finals.'

Sophie pressed her lips together. 'Thanks!'

The sarcasm in her tone must have got through to him, because he frowned and said: 'Now what's the matter? I wasn't being patronising. I think you've got a good chance of making Oxford, don't you?'

Sophie sniffed. 'I don't want to talk about school and examinations! I've just left all that behind!' She moved restlessly and then turned to look at him appealingly. 'How are you, Robert? How long have you been home? And how long are you staying this time?'

Robert concentrated on negotiating the busy late afternoon traffic, but when they reached a quieter thoroughfare, he replied: 'I'm well. And actually, I've been in England a couple of months. I'm working in North Wales at the moment. We're swinging a rail link out across the Sound to the Isle of Cymtraeth.'

'You are?' Sophie's eyes were wide. 'That's marvellous! You must get home practically every weekend.'

Robert's hands tightened on the wheel. 'Not every weekend, Sophie,' he amended dryly. 'I do have other calls on my time.'

Sophie wriggled into a more comfortable position, watching him surreptitiously. He was so cool and aloof. She couldn't get near to him, mentally at least, and her physical attempt hadn't met with much success either.

'How is everyone?' she asked, determinedly trying to

ignore his detachment. 'Are Daddy and Mummy okay? And Simon?' She forced a smile. 'I had a letter from Simon only last week.' She wrinkled her nose. 'Why did you never write to me, Robert? I thought you would.'

Robert ignored her last question and said: 'The parents are fine, and Simon seems quite content to remain at Conwynneth school for the rest of his life.'

'Why not? He's happy there,' commented Sophie thoughtfully. 'He's not restless. Not like you!'

Robert swung past a lumbering wagon. 'Is that what I am?'

'Among other things,' she retorted sourly. 'Well, aren't you? You weren't content to stay in Hereford, were you? I'm sure Simmonds didn't want to lose you.'

Robert shrugged. 'I was offered a better job with more money and the chance to see something of the world before I was too old to enjoy it. I don't see anything particularly restless in that. No doubt you'll feel the same.'

'I shan't!'

'How do you know?'

Sophie stared through the car windows. They were leaving the outskirts of the town behind, climbing into the hills. In spite of the darkening skies the countryside opening up before them was green and beautiful, splashed here and there with the dark clutches of forest which had provided cover for fugitives since the days of the Conqueror. The Welsh Marches! Sophie savoured the words. She might have been born in London, but this was her home, her heritage.

'I'm not the—adventurous type,' she answered him at last. 'I'm basically a home-lover.' She examined her fingernails. 'Of course, if I were to get married, and— and my husband's work took him overseas...'

There was a pregnant pause, and then Robert said

abruptly: 'As a matter of fact, Sophie——'

But he got no further. An ominous rumble of thunder echoed and re-echoed round the hills and he was instantly aware of her stiffening and of the shudder which ran through her.

'You're nervous of storms, aren't you?' he asked quietly. 'Don't be alarmed. You're perfectly safe in the car.'

'I know it. I'm sorry.' Sophie tried to act naturally even though storms had always terrified her. 'Please go on. What were you going to say?'

Robert glanced sideways at her and there was a curious expression twisting his lips. Then he shook his head and said something entirely unexpected: 'Who were those soldiers at the station?'

Sophie gasped. 'No one I knew. I had to stand all the way from Paddington. They shared the same cubbyhole, that's all.' A smile came through. 'They insisted on carrying my cases. I can't imagine why. Can you?'

Robert's expression softened slightly. 'Stop fishing,' he ordered dryly. Then, as a huge globule of rain splashed against the windscreen: 'Well, like it or not, here it comes!'

Within seconds they were engulfed in a torrential downpour that even the efficient wipers found difficult to cope with. Lightning streaked across the sky with a brilliance that artificially illuminated the brooding hills, and a deafening crash of thunder seemed almost completely overhead. Sophie's palms were moist, clasped together in her lap, and she was trying desperately not to give in to the terror which filled her. But suddenly, Robert pulled the car off the road on to a grassy lay-by and releasing his safety belt switched off the engine.

'It's pointless going on in this,' he explained in answer to the silent appeal in her eyes. 'We'd have to crawl, and it won't last long. It's only a summer storm. You should be used to them by now.'

Sophie drew a deep breath. 'I know. I'm a fool.' She trembled as she pressed the release catch of her safety belt and turned sideways in her seat towards him, drawing her legs up under her. His profile was unyielding and yet she had to suppress an almost irresistible impulse to stroke her fingers down his cheek. 'Well, at least it gives us time to talk,' she said rather breathlessly. 'You can tell me what you were going to say.'

'Yes.' Robert leant forward and picked up a pack of Benson and Hedges, putting a cigarette between his lips almost absently. He flicked his lighter, applied the flame to the tip of the cigarette and leaned back in his seat, inhaling deeply.

After a few moments he turned to look at her, his gaze travelling over her intently. Then he took his cigarette out of his mouth and studied the glowing shreds of tobacco with equal intensity. Another rumble of thunder sent the adrenalin rushing through Sophie's veins. Robert's attitude didn't help. She was aware of the tautness in the atmosphere, and wondered that it was that was hardening his jawline. She looked down at her knees and saw that her twisting movements had loosened two buttons on her blouse which, like all her school clothes, was getting too small for her. With burning cheeks her fingers sped to fasten the offending buttons, but her hands trembled so much that they fumbled over the task. A rising sense of emotionalism brought the tears to the backs of her eyes. What was the matter with her? What was the matter with *him*? What had happened to that affinity between them?

With a curt exclamation, Robert had grown tired of watching her unsteady ineptitude, and putting his cigarette between his lips he pushed her fingers aside and tackled the buttons himself.

But before he had the time to fasten them it seemed that everything exploded around them. A shaft of lightning struck a tree only a few yards ahead, splitting its trunk without apparent effort. Overhead the thunder was an ear-rending volume of noise, and the violence of the torrent which fell in a great curtain obscuring all but their most immediate surroundings was drowned as the heavens resounded menacingly.

Sophie trembled uncontrollably and with an oath Robert pulled her towards him, putting his arms around her and pressing her close to his hard warm body.

'Calm down,' he exlaimed, taking the cigarette out of his mouth and pressing it out in the ashtray. 'Everything's going to be all right. Believe me!'

'I'm sorry, Robert,' she whispered huskily, her cheek against the rough texture of his shirt. 'But I hate storms. I'm not pretending. Don't be angry.'

'I'm not angry,' he retorted in exasperated tones, drawing back to look down at her. 'Here, let me fasten those damn buttons.'

She looked up at him as his fingers busied themselves near her midriff and almost against his will her eyes encountered his. He stared down at her for a long disturbing moment and then she covered his hands with hers, stilling their activity, holding them closely against her.

'Sophie!' he protested thickly, trying to pull away, but she held his gaze and reaching up, put her mouth to his. For several agonising moments he resisted, and then his fingers slid beneath her blouse, closing on the firm flesh, propelling her against him with almost desperate urgency. He was trembling now, she could feel it, and his mouth moved on hers, parting her lips, seeking to penetrate the moist sweetness within. Sophie was oblivious to the storm. Her arms were around his neck, touching the smooth skin of his shoulders beneath his shirt, tangling themselves in the thick darkness of the hair on his nape. This was what she had dreamed about—this was where she had longed to be all those months when she had been working at her studies, taking exams, pretending to enjoy the social round of school life. There had been boys there—it was a mixed school. But Sophie's relationships with boys had remained purely platonic and none of them had aroused the slightest interest in her. Yet she only had to see Robert, to touch him, to feel an aching, melting weakness inside her . . .

At last he pushed her away from him, breathing heavily, reaching for his cigarettes and lighting one with none of the precision he had exhibited earlier. He inhaled deeply and then, resting his head back, he said: 'Oh, *God!*' in self-derisory tones.

Sophie ran a hand up to her throat and pulled off the tie which seemed so incongruous after what had just occurred. She folded it and thrust it into the pocket of her blazer. Then she fastened her blouse and tucked it back into her skirt before looking at him again.

'Robert——' she began, but he shook his head.

'Don't say anything,' he commanded, drawing on the cigarette again. 'Don't say anything. Just give me a minute to think straight.' He exhaled unsteadily. 'I knew I shouldn't have allowed your father to persuade me to come and meet you.'

'To—persuade—you?' Sophie stared at him. 'Did you need much—persuasion?'

She sounded hurt and he shook his head impatiently now. 'No—no, I suppose not. God, Sophie—you're my sister——'

'*Step*sister,' she corrected him tautly.

'All right, all right, my stepsister.' Robert raked a hand through his hair, staring out at the unceasing curtain of rain. 'Even so, you know this is—ridiculous!'

'Ridiculous?' Sophie felt unsure of her ground. For a few moments she had been confident that everything was going to be all right, but now ... 'Why is it ridiculous?'

'Don't be naïve, Sophie!' He drew savagely on his cigarette. 'Look, let's get this into perspective, shall we? You—that is, the last time we—were together was that Christmas a couple of years ago when I'd had—too much to drink——'

'That's not true!'

'It is true, Sophie. What other reason could there be for—for what happened?'

'And just now?'

'Yes. Just now.' He ran the back of his hand across his damp forehead. 'I knew I shouldn't have come. I knew—or at least, I guessed what kind of an emotional scene you'd have built up of that incident between us.'

'Incident?'

'Yes, incident, Sophie. For heaven's sake, what do you expect me to call it? You can have no notion of my feelings after—after touching you. I was sick— really sick to my stomach, do you know that? There was I, a supposedly mature and sensible man of twenty-eight, kissing a kid of sixteen——'

'It wasn't like that,' she denied, a little desperately.

'Yes, it was. Just like that.' He raised his eyes heavenward. 'I despised myself utterly.'

'Do you despise yourself now?'

He turned his head to look at her. 'What do you think?'

Sophie moved her shoulders helplessly, feeling the

hot prick of tears behind her eyes. 'I don't know what to think.'

'Don't you?' Robert seemed to be enjoying taunting her. 'My God, Sophie, do you know what you just did?' He uttered a mirthless laugh. 'You're a beautiful girl. That's no excuse, I know, but it does help.'

'Does it?'

'Oh, stop it,' he muttered, straightening to squash out his cigarette in the ashtray. 'You know what you did as well as I do. You're fully aware why those two Army kids offered to carry your cases. I never realised before what a menace you might be.'

'Stop trying to hurt me.'

'Why should I? You don't seem to care who you hurt, do you? Oh, lord, Sophie, stop looking so tragic!' He was gradually recovering his sense of humour. 'All right, I apologise for what happened. I guess it was my fault.'

'Don't talk like that.'

'All right, if you don't want an apology I won't make one. I'm sorry. I was forgetting what a permissive society we live in!'

Her fingers stung across his cheek and she sat in horror staring at the marks of her fingers appearing against the tanned flesh. She caught her breath. 'Oh, Robert,' she exclaimed, starting to cry. 'I'm sorry...'

Robert took a deep breath and expelled it slowly. 'It's all right, Sophie,' he said steadily. 'Look, I think we'd better start all over again, hmm?' He paused. 'You've got rid of all that pent-up emotionalism and I've given myself a—well, we won't go into that. Perhaps your father was right. Perhaps it was as well to come and meet you after all. Get all this foolishness out of your system right at the beginning——'

'My father?' Sophie dried her eyes with the sleeve of her blazer. 'What does my father know about this?

What do you mean?'

Robert sighed. 'Naturally I told him what had happened.'

'You—didn't!'

'Why not? Good God, Sophie, how many more times do I have to tell you? I was sick of myself. I had to give some reason for not coming back to Penn Warren while you were there.'

'But—but—there was that job in the Far East . . .'

'There was no job. At least, not for a couple of months anyway. Sophie, I had to tell him. I was ashamed . . .'

'Ashamed?' Sophie moved her head from side to side. This couldn't be happening—not after—not after the way he had kissed her . . . 'Oh, Robert, I'll never forgive you!'

'I'm not asking for your forgiveness! Hell, I'm just trying to show you the way things really are. I don't want you to go on imagining that what happened that Christmas—well, that it was anything more than a fleeting impulse——'

'It was!' she cried.

Robert shook his head resignedly. 'No, Sophie.' He sighed. 'I thought you were more mature. I was your first—experience, but you certainly weren't mine! And that's all it was, Sophie—an experience.'

'Not for me,' she declared chokingly. 'Oh, I don't know how you can say such things after—after what just happened.'

'Oh, God, Sophie! I'm only human. You invited what just happened, you know you did. I'm not proud of it, but how was I to know——' He broke off and made an impatient gesture. 'I wanted to comfort you, Sophie—because of the storm. I've comforted you before—remember? As I recall it, you once came to my bed in the middle of the night because of a storm. You were about eight years old at the time. You were petrified. I let you stay with me, I put my arms about you—just as I did just now. What happened afterwards was not of my instigation.'

'You're hateful!' she exclaimed in a muffled voice, drawing her knees up to her chin and wrapping her arms round her drawn-up legs. 'I—I never thought you could be so—so cruel, Robert.'

Robert raked his hair back again with a vehemence that spoke of his frustration. He glared out at the storm and made a sound of relief that at last the rain was easing and watery rays of sun were casting spears of rainbow colour across the lake that lay below them in the valley. He leant forward and turned the ignition, breathing a sigh of satisfaction as the powerful engine leapt to instant life. Glancing through the rearview mirror, he drove off the grassy verge and on to the rain-soaked road, controlling the skidding of tyres caked with mud.

'You'd better tidy yourself,' he commented briefly, as they began the descent into the valley. Conwynneth lay in a fold of the hills and already it was possible to see the grey roofs of the cottages that edged the village green. 'Or do you want to have to explain what's been happening?'

Sophie pushed her feet to the floor and fumbled in her pocket for her tie. As she slotted it under the collar of her blouse and fastened it carelessly, her lips were pressed tightly together. She guessed that Robert saw her expression as mutinous. He was not to know that had she not pressed her lips together they would have trembled violently. She felt sick and shaken, and totally unprepared for the confrontation with the family which was to come. All her hopes and fantasies about Robert had been shattered during the last half hour and the last thing she wanted was to have to make any unnecessary explanations. What she really wanted to do was to crawl away somewhere and hide until her wounds had healed a little.

CHAPTER TWO

PENN WARREN was a rambling old house which stood on the outskirts of the village. The Kembles had modernised it to the extent of adding decent plumbing and an efficient central heating system, but much of its atmosphere remained in the oak panelling and wide stone fireplaces. As the boys grew up they constantly seemed to be giving themselves crippling blows on low beams, and yet, for all that, none of them would have had it any different.

To Sophie, it spelled the days of her childhood and adolescence. Long summer days swimming or fishing with the boys, playing cricket or tennis in the huge, partially overgrown garden of the house, autumn with its fires and roasted chestnuts, winter when the snow coated the trees outside and they had all sat round a glowing peat fire drinking mugs of mulled ale. She had always been happy there, and it was doubly hard for her to accept that that happiness had depended so completely on her love for Robert.

She awoke on the morning after her return from school with an unfamiliar feeling of depression causing a dull little ache behind her eyes. She lay for a few minutes wondering what had caused it, and then recollection of the events of the day before came back to her and she rolled on to her stomach, burying her face in the pillow. Oh, God, she thought desperately, what am I going to do?

It had been almost dinner time when she arrived the night before. To her relief, her father was out on a call, and only Laura and Simon had been there to greet her. She thought of Simon with affection. He had been so reassuringly *normal*—so delighted to see her—so good-natured and kind and sweet. He had made things much easier for her, and although at times she had caught him watching her with a rather anxious expression in his eyes, she didn't think her stepmother had noticed anything amiss in her relationship with Robert. By the time her father came home after delivering Mrs. Jones' fourth, the meal was over and Sophie's initial nervousness controlled. Robert had gone out straight after dinner. He had made some excuse about promising to go over to the Hall to see John Meredith, the son of the largest local landowner, who had been at university with him, and no one had demurred. Indeed, if Sophie had not been so wrapped up in her own misery she might have noticed that both her stepmother and Simon relaxed more fully once Robert had left them. Instead, she made a great effort to talk gaily about her last few weeks at school, and she was almost sure she had convinced them that she had no greater problem on her mind than whether or not to apply for university entrance before Christmas.

Now she pushed herself up on her elbows and peered at the Noddy clock ticking away on her bedside table. The clock had been a seventh birthday present from the boys and in spite of its incongruity in her teenage bedroom she had never wanted to change it.

She blinked. It couldn't be half past ten already, could it? Although as she had lain awake for hours listening for the sound of Robert's car and even after his return had been unable to get to sleep for ages, it was possible that she had overslept. But why had no one awakened her? She hunched her shoulders. And why should she want them to anyway? It was better to be asleep and oblivious of what had happened.

However, she could not stay in bed all day. Besides,

she owed it to her parents to pull herself together and act normally. After all, nothing had really changed, that was the amazing thing. Just because her illusions had been shattered did not alter the situation. So far as Robert was concerned, she was still the little sister he had always regarded her.

She forced her mind away from this train of thought. Right now it was almost impossible to accept that never, at any time, had he regarded her in any other light. She would have to accept it, of course, but for the present her most sensible course of action would be to try and behave to him as she had always done. Their relationship had been such a deep and satisfying thing. Surely that had not been destroyed too? Who knows, maybe at some future date he might become attracted to her ...

With a determination she had not known she possessed, Sophie bathed and put on her underwear and was rummaging through her wardrobe for her jeans when there was a knock at the door.

'Who is it?' she called a little breathlessly, and then expelled her breath more steadily as her stepmother's head appeared.

'Oh, you're up!' she exclaimed, pushing open the door and entering the room to reveal a tray laden with fruit juice, ham and eggs, toast and marmalade. 'I was going to give you breakfast in bed. You looked rather tired last night and I told your father you looked as though you could do with a rest.'

Sophie forced a smile. 'I'm fine, really I am. But it was kind of you, Mummy.'

'Well, why don't you put on your dressing gown and pop back into bed?' suggested Laura, making room on the bedside table for the tray. 'It's a dull morning and there's absolutely nothing for you to get up for. Your father won't be back from surgery for another half hour and then you can come down and have coffee with him.'

Sophie hesitated. She wasn't hungry and the prospect of tackling all the food on the tray made her feel slightly sick. But perhaps it was better to hide her lack of appetite up here where she could always dispose of some of it down the lavatory.

'All right,' she agreed, pulling on the frilly flower-sprigged white wrapper which matched the nightdress she had just shed. 'I'll be lazy for once.'

Laura settled the tray across her legs and then stood looking down at her thoughtfully while Sophie manfully swallowed the fruit juice. 'Are you all right, darling?' she asked unexpectedly.

Sophie coloured and almost choked on the grapefruit juice. 'Why—of course,' she managed, clearing her throat. 'Shouldn't I be?'

Laura shook her head. 'Yes, of course.' She paused. 'Graham White came over here last week to enquire when you were due home. I think he's looking forward to seeing you again.'

Sophie put down her glass. 'Graham White? Oh, you mean that boy from Trefyddol.'

'Yes. You know Graham. His father and yours play golf occasionally together.'

'Oh, yes.' Conscious of Laura's gaze Sophie picked up the fork and lifted a tiny button mushroom into her mouth. 'I don't know him awfully well. He's at college, isn't he?'

'Yes. He's just completed his first year.' Laura bit her lip. 'I invited him over next weekend, as a matter of fact. I thought you and he might have a game of tennis together.'

'Oh, *Mummy*!' Sophie couldn't hide her dismay now. 'I can play tennis with Simon and—and Robert!'

'I know that. And I'm sure Simon will be only too

34

willing to give you a game, but Robert may be—rather busy.'

Sophie concentrated her attention on her plate. 'That's all right, I don't mind. I can amuse myself.'

'But you should have friends of your own age, Sophie!' protested Laura. 'You've spent too much time with Simon and Robert.'

Sophie looked up. 'Honestly, Mummy, you don't have to make plans for me. I'm quite capable of entertaining myself.' She moved her shoulders awkwardly. 'Actually, I'm thinking of getting a job.'

The idea had only just occurred to her, but Laura was not to know that, and her stepmother's face assumed an anxious expression.

'A job, Sophie? Oh, I don't think your father would want you to do that.'

'Why not?' It wasn't such a bad idea, after all.

'Well——' Laura spread her hands. 'You've only just finished school. I think he hopes you'll spend this year before you go to university with us.'

Sophie decided she might as well get hanged for a sheep as for a lamb. 'I haven't decided whether I want to go to university yet, Mummy,' she said quietly.

'What? Not go to university?' Laura was horrified. 'Oh, don't be silly, Sophie, of course you're going to university. Your father has great hopes for you. I'm sure you wouldn't dream of letting him down like that!'

Sophie pursed her lips. 'University isn't everything,' she insisted.

'What do you mean?'

'Well, I—I might want to do something else. Get— married, for example.'

'Married?' Laura shook her head impatiently. 'Sophie, you're talking nonsense, and you know it. Good heavens, you're only seventeen! You can't seriously be considering abandoning your studies for—for something as distant as marriage!'

Sophie sniffed. 'As I said, I haven't decided yet.'

'Well, I'm pretty sure if you tell this to your father, he'll be terribly hurt. Sophie, I know he loves the boys —I know he's always treated them as his own sons, but they're not—ultimately. You are his daughter. Surely that must mean something to you. Surely you'll allow him to do for you what he has done for the boys?'

Sophie moved uncomfortably. Laura was right, of course. If she did decide not to go on with her education her father would be very disappointed. Hurt, too, if she was honest.

Sighing, she pushed the tray aside. 'I'm sorry, Mummy, I'm not very hungry right now.'

Laura, who had taken a few steps towards the door, came back to the bed. She looked troubled. 'And I'm sorry, too, Sophie,' she said heavily. 'It's your first morning at home and already I'm upsetting you. I think we'd better leave things as they are for the time being. There's no hurry, whatever you decide.'

Sophie felt suddenly terribly guilty. 'Oh, Mummy!' she exclaimed, and scrambling up on to her knees she hugged the older woman. 'I didn't mean to upset you either.' She drew back to look into her face. 'But I might get a job, you know. Lots of people do. Even— even if it's just until I go to—to university.'

Laura's expression cleared. She looked down at her stepdaughter affectionately. They had always had such a good relationship and she didn't want to spoil that. There had never been any friction between them, any jealousy over Dr. Kemble or the boys. Nothing must change that.

'All right, darling,' she agreed with a smile. 'We'll talk about it. But not yet. Give your father a few days to get used to having you back again. He misses you,

you know.'

Sophie sat back on her heels. 'All right.' She glanced round. 'And now I think I'd better get dressed. I want to go outside and look around. I always enjoy my first few days at home getting used to things again.'

Laura picked up the tray and left her, apparently reassured by Sophie's acquiescence. Sophie took off the frilly wrapper and rescued the denim jeans from the back of her wardrobe. Last summer she had taken a bath in them to shrink them to her body, but now she found they scarcely fitted. She had filled out in all the right places, but the jeans didn't give in the way her skin did. She sighed. They were all she had and they would have to do until she had had time to do some shopping. With a grimace she pulled on a navy blue tee-shirt with a caricature of a once well-loved pop star on the front, and tugged a brush through her long, silvery fair hair.

She encountered Simon on the landing outside his bedroom, and when he saw her he fell back with assumed horror.

'My God!' he exclaimed humorously. 'You don't intend going outside these four walls in those things, do you?'

Sophie wrinkled her nose at him good-naturedly. 'Don't you like the way I look?'

Simon gave a mocking smile. 'Oh, yes, I like it. But I don't somehow think your father will.'

Sophie sighed and pulled impatiently at the tight-fitting pants. 'I can't help it. I shrank them last year and now they're too small.'

'Get your coat and I'll take you into Hereford to buy some more,' suggested Simon reasonably. 'I'm free this morning.'

Sophie was tempted, but she hadn't been downstairs yet. She didn't know what Robert might be doing.

The only thing she could be certain of was that he would surely not ask her to join him.

'I'm not sure...' she began awkwardly, and Simon assumed a tolerant expression. 'Rob's not in,' he commented laconically, and she started at the mention of his name. 'He's gone sailing with John. They arranged it last night.'

'Oh! Oh, I see.' Sophie managed to shrug and walked to the head of the stairs. 'Is Daddy back yet?'

Simon frowned. 'That sounds like his car now.' He paused. 'Shall we go to Hereford?'

Sophie looked back at him. 'All right. If—if you like.' She looked down the stairs as her father's footsteps could be heard on the flags outside the front door. 'But I promised I'd have coffee with Daddy first.'

'Okay.' Simon made her a mock bow and opened his bedroom door. 'I'll be ready in half an hour.'

Simon was right in his assumption that Dr. Kemble would not approve of the revealing jeans. 'You can't go out in those, Sophie,' he exclaimed, as they sat together in his study, companionably sharing a pot of coffee. Laura had tactfully left them alone, and Sophie was almost happy sitting in the huge leather chair opposite her father in the book-lined room she had loved for most of her life.

'Simon says he'll take me to Hereford to buy some more,' she replied, sipping the aromatic beverage with real enjoyment. 'The only thing is...'

She paused and her father laughed. 'I know. You've got no money.'

'How did you guess?' Sophie actually chuckled. 'Actually, Mummy said she would buy me some clothes these holidays. All my things are getting too small for me.'

'I'm not surprised,' remarked Dr. Kemble dryly. 'You're growing up, Sophie. You're quite a young woman now.'

'Yes.' His words had somehow reminded her of Robert's rejection with painful clarity.

If her father noticed her sudden withdrawal, he chose to ignore it, and went on: 'Go into Levinsons. Your mother has an account there. Buy anything you want.'

'Thank you.' Sophie summoned enthusiasm. 'But I shan't buy much today. I'll wait until Mummy can come, too.'

'All right, suit yourself.' Her father was writing a cheque as he spoke. 'Here.' He passed the cheque over to her and she stared at the sum he had written in astonishment.

'But, Daddy——'

'Take it into the bank, deposit it in your own name. I don't want you having to come to me every time you ladder your stockings or need a new lipstick.'

'But, Daddy——' Sophie pointed helplessly at the generous cheque, 'this will keep me in tights and cosmetics for years!'

Dr. Kemble screwed the top on his pen with a smile. 'All the better. But somehow I don't think it will last as long as you imagine. Everything is becoming more expensive, and I don't want my daughter reduced to shopping in discount stores.'

'Oh, Daddy!' Sophie slid off her chair and hugged him closely. 'Oh, Daddy, I do love you!'

'And I love you,' he answered huskily, pulling her down on to his knee, and at once she stiffened. But only for a moment. It was too familiar. The same room —even the same chair! With a choking sob she wrapped her arms round her father's neck and burst into tears.

He allowed her to cry for a few minutes and then he pushed his handkerchief into her hand and said: 'I know all about it—Rob told me. He also told me that you—well, you'd taken it rather badly. Darling, it's only natural. Rob is a very attractive man. Any girl would feel the same. But you've got to get things into perspective. Rob is twelve years older than you are. He has his own life to lead, and you have yours. Now, run along and wash your face and get ready to go with Simon. And—and Sophie——' This as she halted rather stiffly by the door. 'Sophie, don't get any ideas about Simon either, will you, darling?'

Simon's car was a Chrysler station wagon, a much more conventional vehicle than his brother's Jensen, and more suitable to the sometimes rugged country roads. Sophie had changed into a plain short-skirted suit of cream wool, which had been bought for her the previous Easter and was therefore reasonably styled, and an olive green shirt. With her hair secured in a tortoiseshell clasp she looked much older, and Simon looked at her twice as she came to join him in the station wagon.

'Nice,' he commented, as she slid into the seat beside him. 'Are you ready?'

'Hmm.' Sophie looked back at the house to wave at her father and stepmother who had come to see them off. 'Yes, I'm ready. Let's go.'

As Laura had said, it was a dull morning, but gradually the sun was breaking through the clouds, and although it hadn't the humid heat of yesterday, the day was not cool. Simon drove smoothly and after a while Sophie felt her taut nerves relaxing. She brushed a hand across her cheeks. Had Simon noticed that she had been crying? If he had, he wouldn't mention it. Not unless she did.

Hereford was busy with holidaymakers and they had difficulty finding somewhere to park. All the regular car-parks were full, but eventually they managed to squeeze into the kerb between a furniture wagon and a Mini. Simon locked the car and they walked back towards the main thoroughfare where Levinsons occupied a prominent position.

'You don't have to come into the teenage department with me,' Sophie told him, as they rode up in the lift. Levinsons was of the older type of store where escalators were not in evidence.

Simon pushed his hands into the pockets of his denim jacket. 'Don't you want me to?'

Sophie sighed. 'I thought you wouldn't want to.'

'What?' Simon shook his head. 'And have you come out with something like those jeans you were sporting earlier?' he teased.

Sophie felt her lips twitching. 'All right. Thanks, Simon.'

Looking up at him in the close confines of the lift she surprised a rather intense look in his eyes, but then it disappeared and he said lightly: 'That's okay. I'll enjoy the floor-show.'

In the event, Sophie bought two pairs of jeans—one in denim like those she had discarded, and a second pair in yellow corduroy. She also chose a couple of shirts and cardigans and a long cotton skirt which was straight to the knee and then fell in layers of frills to her ankles. Simon approved all her purchases and after they were stowed in the station wagon suggested that they had lunch in town.

'But won't Mummy be expecting us back?' asked Sophie doubtfully.

Simon shrugged. 'I told her we might lunch out. It's a cold meal at home and it won't spoil if we're not there.'

Sophie hesitated. 'All right, she said. 'I think I'd like that, Simon.'

'Good.' Simon took one hand out of his pocket and slid his fingers down over her wrist and between hers. 'Where shall we go?'

They ate in a little Italian restaurant which Simon had discovered some weeks before in a side street just off the market place. There were muted lights and low banquettes beside red-clothed tables, and air-conditioning to keep the place cool. They had poached eggs with anchovies, veal cutlets coated in breadcrumbs and fried in butter, and stuffed peaches soaked in wine. Even Sophie could not resist such appetizing delicacies and she made quite a good meal. She sat back at last, unable to finish her peach, but feeling infinitely better. Simon viewed her warmer complexion with satisfaction and said:

'Did you enjoy it?'

Sophie swallowed the last of her wine and nodded. 'Mmm, it was marvellous!'

'Well, it's the first meal you've eaten since you arrived home,' remarked Simon dryly. 'You only picked at your dinner last night and I saw the breakfast tray that my mother brought downstairs this morning.'

Sophie looked pointedly round the restaurant. 'Has this place been open very long? I don't remember seeing it at Easter.'

'Three months, I believe.' Simon rested his elbows on the table, cupping his chin on his knuckles, watching her. 'Did you know that the parents have arranged for us all to go to France in August?'

'France?' Sophie's head jerked back and she looked at him in surprise. 'No, I didn't know.' She frowned. 'Who—who do you mean by *all*?'

'You, me, Mum and Dad, the Pages——'

'Oh, no!' Sophie groaned. 'Not Vicky Page!'

'And her parents. Mum and Dad have rented a villa in Brittany.' Simon grimaced. 'You should worry. It's

42

me she's after, and everyone knows it. In fact, I'm pretty sure the parents approve. After all, she is the vet's daughter, and she's a local girl. Entirely suitable. Unfortunately, she doesn't suit me.'

Sophie watched sympathetically as he picked up his wine glass and swallowed its contents with the fatalistic confidence of a man about to face a firing squad.

'I suppose they think it's time you were considering settling down,' she ventured comfortably.

Simon's eyes were not grey like his brother's but blue, and they darkened perceptibly as they rested on Sophie's understanding face. 'I think so, too,' he said steadily. 'But not with Vicky Page.'

Sophie could feel the colour flooding into her cheeks and was glad of the muted lights to hide her consternation. But no, she told herself fiercely. She must not imagine such things. Simon wasn't—he *couldn't* be interested in her! Surely her experience with Robert had warned her of the dangers of misinterpreting a situation.

'I—I expect there are plenty of other girls in the village to choose from,' she exclaimed hastily. 'And I mean, Hereford is not far——'

'Sophie!' Simon's hand had slid across the table and covered hers. 'Stop talking nonsense. You know perfectly well what I mean. I'm not interested in the village girls or the Hereford girls or any other girls if it comes to that. It's you I want, and I'm pretty sure you know it.'

'Oh, *Simon!*'

Sophie withdrew her hand from under his and pressed both her hands together tightly in her lap.

Simon shrugged and lay back in his seat. 'That's okay. I know you don't feel the same. But you're too young yet to know what you want.' He drew out a pack of cigarettes and put one between his lips. 'I'm prepared to wait. Just don't try to marry me off in the meantime.'

Sophie shook her head helplessly. 'Oh, Simon,' she said again. 'Why did you tell me?'

Simon lit his cigarette and inhaled deeply. 'You looked pretty down after—well, after speaking with Rob. Look, I know about that, too. Rob told me—he told us all. I was pretty mad at the time, but I've got over it now. These things happen. It's all part of growing up, I guess. I know you've always hero-worshipped Rob, but that was all it was, Sophie, believe me! Rob's too old for you—too experienced. He deserves someone like Emma.'

'Emma? Emma Norton?' Sophie felt slightly sick. So she was still around, was she? She had been right in supposing that Emma would not be so easily discarded as his other girl-friends.

'Well, anyway, let's not talk about that now,' said Simon, summoning the waiter. 'We'll have some more coffee, hmm? And then we'll drive out to the Brecon Beacons, shall we? We can walk for a while and get home in time for tea.' He smiled gently as Sophie began to look doubtful. 'Don't worry, I shan't make a pass at you. At least, not unless you ask me to.'

The Brecon Beacons was a national park that boasted some of the finest hill country in the whole of South Wales. Sophie had come here often with her parents as a child, and once she and Robert and Simon and some of their friends had camped here for a weekend. It was good to get out of the car and stretch their legs and with a fresh breeze clearing the clouds away it was an ideal day for walking. The Beacons themselves, huge peaks of red sandstone, reared their heads in the distance and nearer at hand the splashing waters of one of the numerous falls were cool and inviting. Simon kept to his promise of not touching her and

Sophie relaxed again and enjoyed the outing.

They arrived back at Penn Warren soon after five to find a sleek cream Jaguar parked beside Robert's Jensen on the drive.

'That's John's car,' remarked Simon, in answer to Sophie's questioning glance. 'Do you know John?'

Sophie bit her lip. 'Vaguely, I think. He hasn't been over to the house much while I've been home.'

Simon parked the station wagon and thrust open his door. 'Well, come and meet him. You'll like him. He's engaged to Joanna White. When Emma's here, they all go around in a foursome.' Then, seeing Sophie's suddenly set face, he pressed on: 'You know Joanna, don't you?'

'Is—is that Graham White's sister?'

'Yes, that's right. Oh, yes...' Simon's expression was wry, 'I was forgetting. You made quite a conquest there, didn't you? Old Graham was over here last week asking when you were due home.'

'I know. Mummy told me.' Sophie was grateful to him for leaving the uneasy subject of Emma and Robert. 'She's invited him over next weekend. It's so silly. We only played a few games of tennis together at Easter.'

'It's your irresistible charm,' remarked Simon, with a grin, and indicated that she should precede him into the house.

Robert and John Meredith were in the lounge, learning over the coffee table which was covered with maps. They both looked up when Sophie and Simon appeared in the doorway and immediately both of them rose to their feet.

John Meredith was not so tall as Robert, but he was dark, too, and more stockily built. His smile was slow and attractive, and he left Robert to approach Sophie with open admiration.

'Well, hello, Sophie,' he greeted her warmly. 'It is Sophie, isn't it? It's a cliché, I know, but my! how you've changed.' He had taken her hand and continued to hold it. 'The last time I saw you, you had a ponytail and very short shorts!' His smile widened and his eyes dropped the length of her figure, lingering on her long slender legs. 'Say, maybe that wasn't such a bad idea, after all!'

Sophie couldn't help warming to his personality. 'You're very flattering, Mr. Meredith,' she replied, laughing, 'but I can assure you I never had a ponytail!'

John shook his head. 'It must have been someone else, then. But you did wear the shorts, I remember them.'

'I'm afraid I hardly remember you at all, Mr. Meredith,' said Sophie dauntingly, and he shook his head.

'I have that effect on people. And please—call me John. I'm not quite old enough to be your father, you know.'

Robert's voice broke into their conversation. 'Can we finish what we're doing, John?' he demanded curtly. 'I do have some work to do this evening, you know.'

John grimaced at Sophie and then turned to face her older stepbrother, winking at Simon in the process. 'All right, all right, *bach*. Don't be so impatient. Just because you can talk to this beautiful young creature whenever it suits you to do so——'

'John, please!' Robert looked down at the maps and John released Sophie's hand and crossed the lounge again. But as Sophie and Simon turned to go, Robert looked up again. 'Where have you been, Simon?' he asked.

Simon paused in the doorway, supporting himself against the jamb. 'Here and there.'

46

'Where?'

'We had lunch in Hereford and this afternoon we drove out to the Brecon Beacons.'

'You've been out all day?'

Simon's mouth had hardened. 'Yes. If you'd told me you wanted a report, I'd have compiled one for you.'

Robert's expression was not encouraging. 'Don't you think it would have been more suitable for Sophie to spend her first day at home with her father?' he suggested pointedly.

Sophie's face had flushed and even John was looking a little uncomfortable. But Simon remained cool, if a little tight-lipped.

'I think you should mind your own business,' he told his brother succinctly.

'It is my business,' retorted Robert coldly.

'No, it's not,' returned Simon, equally coldly. 'And if I was you, I'd keep my mouth shut. Or Emma or no Emma, people will begin to think you're jealous!'

There was a moment of silence when Sophie felt sure it could only erupt into violence, when the atmosphere was taut and tense and explosive. And then John, with brilliant timing, said: 'Now, if you've finished, Robert, perhaps we can get on. I, too, have work to do this evening.'

Simon turned away and went through the door and Sophie followed him without looking back. She had never known the brothers react like that to one another before, and it troubled her. She caught up with Simon just before he entered the kitchen. 'Simon?' she appealed, touching his arm.

Simon's face relaxed and he even managed a slight sheepish smile. 'It's all right, Sophie, don't look so worried. Nothing happened.'

'Didn't it?' Sophie didn't believe him.

'No.' Simon sighed, looking down at her resignedly.

'Sophie, I sometimes think that Rob feels he's got himself into a situation he'd rather be out of.'

And with these enigmatic words, he opened the kitchen door.

CHAPTER THREE

THE next two weeks were hectic ones. Dr. Kemble found he had an unexpected spate of measles and mumps on his hands and Sophie went down to the surgery in the village with him most mornings to help Mrs. Lewis, his nurse, dispense pills and medicines. She was glad of the occupation to take her mind from other things, and it meant she saw more of her father and less of her two stepbrothers. Robert was apparently taking some holiday before returning to his work in North Wales, but he was out of the house a lot and Sophie hadn't the courage to ask where he went or what he was doing. Simon, on the other hand, seemed quite content to laze around, enjoying the break from school, although more often than not he would appear at the surgery around coffee time and make some outrageous excuse about enjoying Mrs. Lewis's particular blend.

Towards the end of the second week, Simon had to go into Hereford for his mother, and that morning Sophie left the surgery earlier than usual to walk back to the house. She had not, as yet, had much time to renew her acquaintanceship with the village and she enjoyed strolling across the village green and feeding some biscuit crumbs to the ducks on the pond. Conwynneth was a most attractive place to be on a warm summer morning, the cottages around the green vying with one another to see which of them could produce the most colourful setting. The gardens were bright with roses and delphiniums, sweet peas and geraniums, climbing plants framing open doorways, lupins and sunflowers bright against thick laurel hedges.

Sophie felt an almost overwhelming sense of well-being and wondered how the Roman scholar Tacitus could have considered Britain's climate to be: 'objectionable, with frequent rains and mists...'

She was walking up the uneven road with its high leafy hedges towards her father's house when a car slowed behind her and presently pulled alongside her. It was sleek and cream, and to her surprise she recognised John Meredith at the wheel.

'Hello, Sophie,' he said, leaning out of his window, his eyes eloquent with the pleasure he got from looking at her slender, yet rounded, body encased in the new corded jeans and a paler yellow shirt.

'Hello, Mr. Meredith,' she answered, stopping and shading her eyes against the glare of the sun. 'Isn't it a lovely morning?'

'Beautiful,' he agreed, but he wasn't looking at the day.

Sophie moved uncomfortably. 'I'm just on my way home. It's so hot and I'm dying for a long cold drink.'

'That sounds like an invitation,' he remarked, opening his door. 'I could do with a long cold drink, too.'

Sophie flushed. 'Oh, I didn't mean—that is——' She broke off. 'Of course, if you'd like a lager, I'm sure my mother would be only too pleased to provide you with one.'

John shook his head. 'I'm sorry, I phrase myself badly. What I really meant was—would you allow me to buy you a drink?'

Sophie began to shake her head. 'I'm not eighteen——'

He smiled. 'My home is not too far away. Come back with me and share a beer.' He paused. 'Wouldn't you like a swim? My father installed a pool just last year.'

Sophie didn't know what to say. His invitation was very tempting, but she hardly knew him. The fact that

Robert did was no recommendation.

'I'd—have to ask my mother,' she said at last.

'All right.' John was agreeable. 'Get in the car and I'll take you the last few yards. You can collect your swim-suit at the same time.'

'You're very sure she'll allow me to come, aren't you?' commented Sophie dryly, after he had helped her into the seat beside him.

John grinned at her. 'Why not? If my invitation was suspect, I'd hardly take you to the Hall, would I?'

Sophie had to concede that this was so, and in a very short time she was slipping out of the Jaguar and running up the steps into the house. Mrs. Forrest, her stepmother's daily, was polishing the panelling in the hall and Sophie halted and said: 'Where's Mummy, Mrs. Forrest?'

'She's gone into Hereford with Master Simon, miss. She wasn't going to go and then she decided at the last minute she would. Why? Was it something important for your father?'

Sophie heaved an impatient sigh. 'What? Oh, no, no. Not important.' She chewed unhappily at her lip. 'Is—is Robert in?'

'No, miss. I've got the house to myself. Have you had some coffee, or would you like me to make some?'

'Oh, no. I—er—I had coffee with my father at the surgery.' Sophie hunched her shoulders. 'No, as a matter of fact, I just came back for my swim-suit.'

'Your swim-suit, miss!' Mrs. Forrest shook her head. 'You going sunbathing? You want to watch your skin. Don't you go getting burned now.'

The decision made, Sophie ran lightly up the stairs. 'I won't, Mrs. Forrest,' she called, going into her bedroom.

When she climbed into the car a few minutes later, she was wearing her navy blue bikini beneath her shirt and jeans and carrying a towel.

'All right?' asked John, raising his eyebrows.

Sophie hesitated. 'Yes, all right,' she nodded.

She had never been to the Hall before and it was quite an exciting prospect. She had heard about it, of course. The Merediths were regarded as the local squires and their activities always made news. But visiting the Hall for herself was something else, and she looked about her with interest after John had let them through the barred gate which gave access to the parkland surrounding his home.

The Hall itself was a mellow stone building reflecting the architectural styles of various periods. Its original foundations had been laid in the late seventeenth century, but successive owners had added to it and distorted its appearance so that now it owed allegiance to no particular period. For all that, it was an attractive building with lots of stores and outbuildings rambling into the copse of elms which formed its backcloth.

John parked the car to one side of the house and when Sophie climbed out he was standing beside her.

'This way,' he said, leading her along a path edged by rhododendron bushes that curved round to the back of the house. 'It sounds as though Veronica and her friends are already using the pool.'

Sophie felt the first twinges of reluctance. She had never met Veronica Meredith, and the prospect of joining John's sister and a group of people she didn't know was a daunting one.

'Perhaps I should go . . .' she began awkwardly, but John turned back and caught her hand.

'Why?' he challenged. 'You're not afraid of meeting people, are you?'

'No, but——' Sophie gestured helplessly. It was difficult to say that her position was bound to be suspect. She was not his fiancée for one thing, and therefore had no right to be with him. 'What about Joanna?' she managed, at last.

John smiled his slow smile. 'Let me worry about Joanna, hmm?' he suggested gently, and drew her after him until they emerged on to a bright, sunlit patio.

The kidney-shaped pool was blue-tiled and the water glinted brilliantly. Several young people were splashing about in the pool, and striped li-los and colourful garden furniture set about its rim gave the scene a continental appearance. John was recognised and greetings were called to him, while Sophie was conscious of being scrutinised rather closely.

'A drink first,' commented John, releasing her hand to walk across to a trolley set in the shade of the terrace that ran along the back of the house. He glanced round and indicated that she should join him. 'What will you have? Lager; shandy; beer; a Coke?'

Sophie looked down at the array of bottles nestling in a bed of ice. 'Oh—Coke, I think.'

John continued to smile at her as he hooked the lid of a Coke bottle under the automatic lever and handed the opened bottle to her. 'Straws or glasses?' he asked.

'I think I can manage,' replied Sophie, unable to resist smiling in return, and John nodded and hooked off the lid of a beer, putting the bottle to his lips and drinking thirstily.

Sophie was copying his example when she became aware that a girl, some years older than herself, and dripping water from red-brown hair and a cream bikini, had climbed out of the pool and was approaching them. She looked curiously at Sophie, allowed a small smile of welcome, and then turned to John.

'Well?' she said pointedly, 'and what have you been doing?'

John threw his empty bottle into the trash can. 'Oh,

hello, Ronnie,' he responded easily. 'Allow me to introduce you to Rob's sister, Sophie. Sophie, this is my sister Veronica.'

Veronica held out a wet hand, grimaced and withdrew it. 'Sorry, I'm soaking. Hello, Sophie. You're just home from school, aren't you?'

'I've finished school,' stated Sophie rather flatly.

'Oh, have you?' Veronica's tone indicated that she didn't look as though she should be. She glanced round. 'Well, you know the gang, don't you, John? You can introduce Sophie around.' She paused. 'By the way, Joanna rang earlier. I think she expected you to be taking her to lunch or something.'

John's lips twitched. 'Are you sure about that, Ron?'

To Sophie's astonishment, Veronica coloured. 'Well, she did ring,' she declared irritably. 'I expect she'll ring again.'

'I expect she will,' agreed John amiably, and took Sophie's empty bottle from her unresisting fingers. He looked at her steadily and said: 'Are you ready for a swim now, or do you want another drink?'

Sophie glanced awkwardly at Veronica and with an impatient exclamation the other girl walked away. Sophie looked after her anxiously. 'I don't think your sister approves,' she murmured uncomfortably.

John put out his hand and tugged gently at a strand of her silky hair. 'Do you know something?' he asked. 'I don't particularly care.'

The other guests were less concerned with John's behaviour. Playing in the pool was fun, and although initially the water felt ice-cold in no time at all Sophie's heated body got used to it. Names were casually thrown around, and occasionally Sophie would find herself being chatted up by others of the young men. She enjoyed the friendly banter and found herself able to parry most of their comments. She had always moved in a mixed company and didn't find it difficult talking to the opposite sex.

Her hair was soaking and she had no idea of the time when she became aware of a tall figure standing on the patio watching them, a lean dark man dressed in an immaculate slate grey suit, whose tanned features were set and uncompromising. It was Robert, and at once Sophie's new-found confidence deserted her. John had apparently seen him, too, because he was climbing out of the pool and walking across to him.

'Hi, Rob!'

'You coming to join us?'

The friendly comments floated across the water to him, but he didn't answer them. He was talking to John and watching them Sophie sensed the same kind of aggression she had felt between him and Simon.

'I don't think your brother approves of John bringing you here,' remarked a sardonic voice in her ear, and turning, Sophie found Veronica just behind her.

She shrugged with what she hoped was casual inconsequence. 'I can't imagine why.'

'Can't you?' Veronica gave her an old-fashioned look. 'You know John's engaged, don't you? Would you like your fiancé playing around with someone else?'

Sophie gasped, 'John and I were not—playing around!'

Veronica shrugged. 'I know my brother better than you do, Sophie. I saw the way he was looking at you. Believe me, John's interested.' She grimaced. 'Perhaps I shouldn't have told you, but—well, I don't think you're the type to take advantage of the fact.'

Sophie struggled to climb out of the pool. 'Thank you,' she managed in a choking voice, and endeavoured to walk across to where her towel was lying without looking in Robert's direction. But John saw her and called her, and wrapping the towel round her shoulders Sophie approached the two men. She concentrated her attention on John and tried not to feel intimidated by the angry expression on Robert's face.

'I'm afraid you have to go. Sophie,' said John regretfully. 'Big brother's come for you. I've just been trying to convince him that I didn't intend to kidnap you. He says that you didn't tell anyone where you were going.'

'Oh!' Sophie had to look at Robert then and she flinched from the coldness in his eyes. 'Well, there was no one to tell. Mummy had gone to Hereford with Simon and Daddy was still at the surgery.'

'You could have mentioned your whereabouts to Mrs. Forrest,' retorted Robert curtly. 'Do you realise I've been looking for you for the past hour? Your father is worried sick. Fortunately my mother and Simon are not yet back from Hereford or they'd have been anxious, too. You really are the most inconsiderate little madam I've ever had the misfortune to meet!'

Sophie's cheeks were pale now and John looked from one to the other of them with obvious discomfort. 'I say, Rob,' he mumbled, 'that's a bit strong, isn't it?' He moved restlessly. 'If anyone's to blame, it's me. I invited Sophie here.'

Robert took a deep breath, controlling his temper. 'Get your clothes on, Sophie,' he said. 'We're leaving.'

Sophie hesitated only a moment, and then scurried across to the bathing cubicles which ran along one side of the pool. She had left her clothes there earlier and with careless haste she rubbed her body damp dry and then put them on. She was wringing out the scanty bikini as she walked back to where her stepbrother was still talking to John. She rung out her hair, too, but trickles of water still persisted in running down her neck. 'I'm ready,' she said tautly.

'Good.' Robert nodded to John and began to walk towards the path which led round to the front of the building, but John caught Sophie's arm, detaining her for a moment.

'I'm sorry,' he said, looking into her eyes apologetically.

'It's not your fault.'

'Not altogether perhaps, but then who would have thought Rob could get so uptight about it?' He shrugged. 'When can I see you again?'

Sophie realised that Robert had halted at the corner and was standing watching them. 'You can't be serious!' she gasped.

'Why not?'

Why not indeed? Sophie shook her head. 'I must go.' She drew her arm out of his grasp.

'Can I give you a ring?' he persisted.

Sophie gave him a troubled look. 'I—I—oh, I suppose so,' she agreed, and hurried after Robert feeling as though the Sword of Damocles was about to fall.

Robert's car was parked beside the Jaguar and he was already seated inside when Sophie reached it. She opened the door and got in quickly and he thrust the gear into drive and spun the wheel with a screaming scrunch of tyres on the gravelled forecourt. He didn't speak until they reached the park gate and then he said: 'Will you open the gate, please?' in controlled tones.

'Open it yourself!' retorted Sophie, staring blindly out of the window at her side.

Robert stood on his brakes and because she hadn't fastened her seat belt she was almost ejected through the windscreen. She managed to save herself and stared at him angrily as he pushed open his door and got out. He drove the car through the gate, and then got out again and secured it.

By this time Sophie's initial bout of recklessness had subsided, and she half wished she had opened the gate for him. After all, if her father had been worried...

'I'm sorry if you've been put to any inconvenience on my account,' she managed through tight lips. 'I'm sorry if Daddy was worried. But that doesn't give you the right to speak to me like that in front of—of a stranger!'

Robert said nothing. He drove out on to the narrow country road and accelerated towards the village. Sophie stared at him mutinously. He looked so dark and cool and attractive while she was hot and dishevelled. She felt the brevity of her years and when compared to his sophistication and wondered how she had ever dared to provoke him as she had two weeks ago coming home from the station.

'What do you want me to say?' she burst out at last, unable to bear the tense silence any longer.

Robert glanced at her. His lashes were long and thick and veiled the coldness of his eyes. He seemed remote—detached. Had she really once shared his bed in a storm? Been gathered close against his hard warm body with love and affection? It didn't seem possible, the way he was looking at her now.

He had returned his attention to the road and already the outskirts of the village were coming into view, the tall hedges around Penn Warren hiding the house from sight. 'I don't particularly want you to say anything,' he replied tersely. 'Just don't disappear like that again without telling anyone where you're going!'

Sophie hunched her shoulders. 'Such a fuss!'

'And I shouldn't get involved with John Meredith either,' went on Robert, as though she hadn't spoken. 'He has a fiancée, and she conceivably might object.'

'I know that. I'm not a child!' she declared resentfully.

Robert's second sweeping glance was eloquent with meaning and she wanted to cry.

'Why—why do you have to be so horrible to me all the time?' she exclaimed defensively. 'We—we used to be friends!'

Robert turned the Jensen between the drive gates and drew up before the house. Sophie's breathing was shallow and jerky and she turned at once to get out. She wanted to put as much distance between them as possible. But the door would not open and she shook it with tremulous impatience, starting when he said laconically: 'It's locked.'

She turned to look at him then. 'Will you please open it?'

'In a minute.' Robert drew a deep breath, and almost against his better judgement, he said: 'I apologise, Sophie. I shouldn't have spoken to you as I did in front of John. Put it down to—over-reaction, if you like. I'm sorry.'

Sophie felt so relieved, she was lightheaded. 'Th—that's all right, Robert,' she forgave him unsteadily, wishing he would look at her instead of staring straight ahead.

He turned then, one hand resting on the back of her seat. He was unsmiling, but the cold hardness had gone from his expression. 'I'm—I've got to go to Gloucester this afternoon. Would you like to come?'

Sophie's mouth felt dry. 'Do you want me to?'

His lips twisted wryly. 'I shouldn't have asked you otherwise, should I?'

She bent her head, and her wet hair falling about her ears made her conscious of her appearance. 'I—I'm such a mess,' she said, not quite knowing why she said it.

'Don't you want to come?' he demanded shortly.

She looked up at him then, her green eyes wide and luminous. 'You know I do.'

Robert looked at her for a long shattering moment and then he swung round in his seat and pushed open his door. 'Then I suggest you stop talking rubbish and go and get ready. We'll leave straight after lunch.'

Sophie's father was surprised to find she had been at the Hall, but to her relief he seemed to think she had been chastised enough. He made some comment about always telling someone where she was going and then went into his study to enjoy his pre-lunch sherry.

Simon and Sophie's stepmother arrived back while Sophie was drying her hair and she hurried and dressed in a plain, sleeveless cotton jersey and the long cotton skirt she had bought in Hereford.

Robert told the family over lunch that he and Sophie were going to Gloucester that afternoon and the news was received with very mixed feelings. Sophie's stepmother was cautiously enthusiastic, her father was clearly doubtful, and Simon was downright antagonistic to the idea.

'I was going to suggest taking Sophie to the coast this afternoon as it's such a hot day,' he decided irritably. 'What on earth is she going to do in Gloucester? Towns are not the places to spend afternoons like this! She'd enjoy the beach and swimming far better, wouldn't you, Sophie?'

Before Sophie could reply, however, Robert said: 'As Sophie went swimming this morning, she might enjoy a change of scene, don't you think?' in cool sardonic tones.

'Sophie ... went swimming ...'

Simon was clearly confused and even her stepmother was looking surprised. 'I went to the Hall,' said Sophie hastily. 'I—er—I met John Meredith when I was walking home from surgery. He—he invited me.'

Simon looked stunned. 'You didn't tell me.'

'I've hardly had the opportunity.'

'But why should John invite you to the Hall?' exclaimed Laura.

Robert gave his mother an old-fashioned look. 'You don't really need an answer to that, do you?'

Laura shrugged and looked at her husband. 'But Sophie's so—young!'

'She'll be eighteen in November,' pointed out Simon impatiently. 'You can hardly regard someone who's considered old enough to vote as just out of the schoolroom, can you?'

'Even so...' Laura shook her head. 'And in any case, John's engaged.'

'Being engaged doesn't necessarily deprive a man of his sight, Laura,' remarked Dr. Kemble, looking piercingly at Robert. Then he pushed his chair from the table. 'And now, if you'll all excuse me, I'm going to take my coffee into the study. I'm going to have forty winks before I go over to High Apsdale. I promised Martin Evans I'd go and have a look at Doris. She doesn't like coming into the surgery, and he's a bit worried about her blood pressure again. She's doing too much, as usual, I suppose. These hill farmers—they certainly earn their living.'

After her father had left the table, Sophie began collecting the dirty plates together. 'I'll do these,' she offered, but Laura shook her head.

'No, don't bother. Mrs. Forrest can help me with them later.' She looked across at her elder son. 'You're leaving now?'

'In about five minutes, yes,' agreed Robert, rising to his feet and leaving the room. After a minute Simon got up, too, and followed him and Sophie looked helplessly at her stepmother.

'What should I do?'

Laura shrugged. 'Go with Robert, of course. You've said you will, haven't you?'

'Yes, but——'

'Just remember about Emma,' Laura interrupted her, and picking up the two serving dishes she carried them out to the kitchen.

After she had gone, Sophie stared broodingly down at the table. Now what had her stepmother meant by that? She pressed her lips together. Surely Robert wasn't seriously involved with Emma Norton, was he?

She left the table and walked across the room to gaze moodily out across the lawns at the back of the house. Simon had told her that Robert and Emma went around in a foursome with John Meredith and his girl-friend. Had he been trying to tell her that Robert was thinking of getting engaged, too? Was that the reason Robert had choked her off so cruelly when she had revealed her own foolish fantasies? Her throat felt tight. Robert couldn't be thinking of marrying Emma Norton! She wasn't his type at all!

'Are you ready?'

Robert's cool question took her by surprise and she swung round almost guiltily to find him standing in the open doorway. He had shed the jacket of his suit and had it draped over one shoulder, his thumb hooked into its collar. The close-fitting trousers moulded his lean hips, the powerful muscles of his thighs firm against the fine cloth. He looked dark and disturbingly attractive, the sombreness of his expression adding to rather than detracting from her intense awareness of him.

She looked down awkwardly at the long cotton skirt and close-fitting apricot jersey. Beside his casual elegance she felt uncomfortably aware of her own limitations, and with a sigh, she said: 'Do I look all right?'

Robert's mouth turned down at the corners. 'Of course.'

Sophie sighed. 'Are you sure? Where are we going? Ought I to wear something more formal?'

'Come on, Sophie!' Impatience coloured his tone now. 'I don't have all day.'

'Well, perhaps you'd better go on your own, then!' Sophie retorted, stung by his indifference.

Robert came right into the room and put his fingers firmly round her wrist. 'You look fine,' he said forcefully. 'I like the skirt. It suits you. Now, will you come?'

Sophie was smiling up at him when she became aware that Simon had come to stand in the doorway. His face was grim and he thrust his hands belligerently into his pockets.

'You're going, then?' he said. It was more of a statement than a question.

'Yes, we're going,' said Robert, retaining his hold on Sophie's wrist. 'If you have no objections, of course.'

'I have plenty,' retorted Simon, blocking the doorway. 'Like just what kind of game do you think you're playing?'

'Oh, Simon, please...'

Sophie felt terrible. This was twice in one day she had been the bone of contention between Robert and another man. She had never dreamt that life could suddenly be so complicated.

'Shift yourself, Simon.' Robert's tone was dangerously quiet.

'And if I don't?' Simon was aggressive.

'What on earth is going on here?' Laura's light tones had never been so welcome to Sophie's ears. His mother propelled Simon aside and said: 'Are you leaving now, Robert? Remember the Pages are coming for dinner, won't you? They haven't seen Sophie since she came home.'

There was a moment when Sophie thought that Robert was about to continue with the argument with his brother, and then his fingers on her wrist relaxed, and she felt the blood pouring back into her numbed hand.

'We won't be late,' he promised evenly. 'See you!' And with Robert propelling Sophie before him they left the room.

CHAPTER FOUR

SOPHIE found her knees were trembling when she got into the car and was glad of the long skirt to hide them. She would never have believed that Simon—easy-going, amiable Simon—should behave so completely out of character. Robert—well, Robert was a different proposition. He had always been a little unpredictable, and she, perhaps more than anyone, should not be shocked at the strength of his ruthlessness.

Robert swung the powerful car out of the drive and accelerated through the village, turning in the opposite direction from that which she and Simon had followed to Hereford. Once the environs of the village had fallen behind them, he reached for a pack of cigarettes and put one between his teeth, lighting it from the switch on the dash. Only then did she notice that his hands were not entirely steady, and the knowledge was reassuring. She didn't like to think of the brothers quarrelling over her.

The car windows were open and a breeze blowing through was very welcome. Sophie lay back in her seat and tried to relax, raising one hand to lift the weight of her hair from her neck. Ahead the road shimmered with heat, and she sighed. She was with Robert, they had the whole afternoon ahead of them. Why shouldn't she be content? Why did she feel so distrait?

Her movements attracted Robert's attention, and he glanced down at her briefly. Then returning his attention to the road, he said: 'What's with you and Simon? What has he been telling you about me?'

Sophie was shocked. 'I don't think he's told me anything about you,' she answered, wriggling into a more upright position inside the safety belt.

'No?' Robert sounded sceptical. 'Then what has he told you about himself?'

Sophie stared at him for a moment and then meeting his grey eyes looked away. 'What could he tell me?'

Robert shook his head, dragging viciously at his cigarette. 'He's not your keeper, is he?'

'What's that supposed to mean?' she asked indignantly.

'I don't like the way he behaves towards you. As though he was personally responsible for your welfare.'

'You gave a pretty good imitation of that yourself this morning,' Sophie retorted coldly. 'You're not my keeper either.'

There was an uneasy silence for a few minutes and she saw his irritation manifest itself in the way he squashed out the half-smoked cigarette. He lit another almost absently, and then said grimly: 'I don't want you getting emotionally involved with Simon!'

Sophie was astonished at his audacity. 'I don't think it's any of your business!' she declared tremulously.

Robert slanted her a sidelong glance. 'I shall make it so.'

Sophie drew a trembling breath. 'And I suppose that applies to John Meredith, too?'

'Of course.'

'Of course.' Sophie mimicked his tone. 'And, *of course*, you will let me know when you find someone suitable for me to get emotionally involved with, won't you?' she taunted him scornfully.

'I've told you—you're too young to get involved with anyone,' he snapped. 'Oh, for God's sake, Sophie, you can't think of having—well, having a relationship with Simon!'

'Did I say that I did?'

His jaw tautened. 'No. But I know how Simon feels about you.'

'Ought you to be telling me that?' she flared.

'Why not? He's already told you himself, hasn't he?'

'How do you know?'

Robert braked violently as the road wound treacherously back on itself. 'Because he told me,' he retorted angrily.

'I see.' Sophie looked down at her hands. 'Well, whatever I decide to do, you're not involved, are you? You have—Emma, haven't you?'

Robert's face was savage. 'Who told you that?'

Sophie registered his fury and then returned her attention to hands that were trembling again. 'Does it matter? It's true, isn't it? You're thinking of getting engaged to her, aren't you?'

'Thinking of—getting engaged——' Robert repeated her words incomprehensively, and then gathered his thoughts. 'I'd rather not discuss that right now, if you don't mind.'

'Oh, no.' Sophie looked up at him contemptuously. 'I'm not permitted to question you, is that it? You want it all your own way, Robert.' She hid the pain he had inflicted by not denying her words in anger. 'Well, I shall do whatever I like, do you understand? And if—if your friend John Meredith asks me to go out with him again, I shall go!'

The silence between them stretched for miles, and Sophie rested her head back wearily. Why had she agreed to come out with him? She should have known better. It seemed it was impossible now for them to be together without spending the whole time deliberately hurting one another. At least, he hurt her. She wasn't so sure of her own success.

At last, when she was wondering whether he was

considering turning back and abandoning the outing, he said heavily: 'Look, we've got the afternoon ahead of us. Shall we try and behave like civilised human beings and be polite to one another for a change? I don't think I can stand much more of this!'

Sophie looked at him with feigned indifference, while the words she spoke tore at her emotions. 'Wouldn't you rather go back?'

Robert looked at her then, and taking one hand from the wheel allowed his fingers to close over her knee through the thin material of her skirt. 'No,' he said steadily. 'I don't want to go back.'

'Oh, Robert!'

Sophie felt near to tears and she put her hand over his until his fingers moved and twined themselves with hers. He didn't look at her again, but he drove the rest of the journey one-handed.

Gloucester, like Hereford, attracted tourists, all eager to explore the ancient aspects of the city. Gabled and timbered houses, and some of the old inns preserved the atmosphere of Elizabethan England, while the basically Norman cathedral reflected every style of Gothic architecture. Sophie had spent many happy hours in the cathedral, exploring the chapels and cloisters, examining the shrines of famous people buried there.

Robert parked the car in the multi-storey park near the cathedral and when they emerged into the sunshine again, he said: 'I have to visit the company office in Henry Street, Sophie. It wouldn't be much fun for you. Could you entertain yourself for about an hour and then we'll go and have afternoon tea, if you like.'

Sophie could hardly hide her disappointment. Since leaving the car, Robert had made no attempt to touch her, and now it seemed he was to abandon her. 'All right,' she agreed without enthusiasm, and he put out

68

a hand and touched her cheek.

'Stop looking like that,' he commanded, almost impatiently. 'There's a very good second-hand bookshop near the cathedral. I guarantee if you make your way there, I'll be back before you miss me.'

Sophie's mouth lifted slightly at the corners. 'Want to bet?'

Robert looked as though he was about to say something more and then abruptly he turned away. 'Okay,' he said briskly. 'I'll see you in Rhymers at half past four. Be good!'

And with a slight nod of his head he strode away.

As it happened, Sophie bumped into one of her old school friends in Rhymers. Sally Vincent lived in Gloucester, but she had left school the previous Christmas and the two girls had lost touch with one another.

'I say, this is marvellous!' she exclaimed, cornering the younger girl between the bookshelves. 'We must exchange addresses, Sophie. I've been meaning to give you a ring ever since I left, but you know how it is...'

'Yes,' Sophie smiled. 'I——'

'Well, I've been abroad, actually. Mummy has a distant cousin who married an Austrian businessman, and I've been staying with them. It was terrific. Have you ever been to Austria?'

'No, but——'

'The seasons run into one another, you know. Winter sports, skiing, that sort of thing, and then it's so deliciously hot in the summer! You've finished school now, haven't you, Sophie? Have you decided what you're going to do?'

Sophie did manage to get a word in here and there. She found Sally's apparently unending fund of gossip a relief after the tension earlier, and by the time Robert returned they had exchanged addresses and telephone numbers, and Sally had decreed that Sophie simply must attend one of their barbecue parties soon. Robert came, shouldering his way through the book addicts thronging the shelves of the busy shop, and frowned when he saw that Sophie was no longer alone. Sally, on the other hand, stared admiringly at her friend's escort, and nudging Sophie said: 'Aren't you going to introduce me, poppet?'

Sophie performed the introductions reluctantly. Sally was a very attractive girl and a shaft of pure jealousy tore through her when Sally realised exactly what their relationship was. A gleam of speculation came into her eyes and she chatted to Robert wittily, using all her undoubted charm. Robert's frown disappeared, and he seemed relaxed and amiable. But Sophie felt completely superfluous from the moment he appeared.

'I say,' Sally exclaimed at last, 'why don't you and your—er—stepbrother come back to my house for dinner this evening, Sophie? There's only Mummy and Daddy and me for once, and I'm sure my father would welcome some intelligent conversation. My escorts tend to be either completely servile or boringly left-wing. He usually avoids them, as you can imagine.' She laughed into Robert's eyes. 'Do say you'll come.'

'I'm afraid we can't,' replied Robert apologetically, before Sophie could say anything. 'Our parents are expecting guests this evening, and we've promised to be back.'

'Oh, that's a pity!' Sally looked disappointed. Then she brightened. 'Still, I've got Sophie's phone number. Perhaps some other time.'

'Perhaps so.' Robert was non-committal, much to Sophie's relief.

'Well, anyway,' went on Sally undaunted, 'it's been so nice seeing you again, Sophie. We mustn't lose touch.'

'No.' Sophie was less enthusiastic now.

'I'm afraid we must be going,' said Robert, putting a hand beneath Sophie's elbow, his touch sending ripples of anticipation up her arm.

'Oh, must you?' Sally sighed. 'Well, never mind. I'll give you a ring soon, Sophie. I'm looking forward to talking over more old times.' But her eyes lingered on Robert and Sophie wondered rather cynically whether she would have remained as enthusiastic if Robert hadn't appeared on the scene.

Farewells were made and Sophie and Robert threaded their way outside again. Once there, Robert expelled his breath noisily, and said: 'It was damned oppressive in there, wasn't it?' He had put on his jacket to visit his office and now he ran one finger round the inside of his shirt collar. 'How did you stand it for almost an hour!'

'Oh, I—Sally was talking.' Sophie made a vague gesture. 'I didn't notice.'

'Sally does a lot of talking, doesn't she?' he commented dryly, beginning to walk towards the main street.

Sophie glanced up at him. 'Do you think so?'

'Well, don't you? Or didn't you notice that either?'

Sophie shrugged. 'I suppose so. She's a very vivacious person.'

'You think?'

'Of course.'

Robert raised his eyes heavenward. 'All right, if you say so.'

'I should have thought you'd have appreciated that.'

'Why?' Robert uttered an amused snort. 'Because she made a play for me?' He shook his head at her shocked face. 'Stop being so prickly! If you like her, okay. I can't be expected to like everybody.'

Sophie's lips quivered. 'I thought you did.'

'What? Like everybody—or just her?'

'Just—her.'

He found her hand then, linking his fingers with hers as Simon had done but with infinitely more pressure. 'Oh, Sophie,' he said resignedly, 'I know a hundred girls exactly like her. The London office is full of them. She's no novelty, believe me!'

And Sophie did. She looked up at him with her heart in her eyes and with a muttered oath, he said: 'Let's have some tea, eh?' and quickened his step.

But by this time all the restaurants and cafeterias were overflowing with customers and after twenty minutes Robert looked at his watch and said: 'Look, this is hopeless. How about buying some cans of beer or Coke and a couple of sandwiches and driving somewhere out of town to eat them?'

'Mmm, super!' exclaimed Sophie eagerly, and leaving her Robert entered the nearest bakery.

He emerged carrying two bags and four cans, and Sophie relieved him of two of the cans before making their way back to the car-park.

It was good to get out of town and Robert seemed in no hurry to get back. They found a place to park the car on the roadside and then left it to scramble down a bank to where a narrow stream meandered its way towards the River Severn. Robert had shed his jacket again, and his tie, and dropping his burden he stretched out lazily on the lush green grass.

'This is better than some stuffy café,' he murmured contentedly. 'It's years since I had a picnic.'

Sophie was opening the two paper bags. Inside one were half a dozen bread rolls filled with an assortment of things like chicken, ham, egg, cheese and tomato, while the other contained two sticky cream cakes. She smiled, recognising her own particular favourite. She wouldn't have expected him to remember.

Robert propped himself up on one elbow. 'Help yourself,' he advised lazily. 'Just give me a sandwich. Anything you like.'

Sophie, whose appetite had not been helped by the contretemps at lunch time, enjoyed the alfresco meal, munching contentedly, gazing across the stream at a herd of dairy cows grazing in the meadow. The only sounds were the calling of the birds, an occasional insect buzzing about them, and the infrequent swish of a car passing on the road above them. They didn't have to talk. Just being with Robert in this mood was enough.

Finally Robert reached for a can of beer and tearing off its tab drank deeply. Then he dropped the empty can on to the grass beside him and stretched out again.

Sophie drank a can of Coke, and then gathered the empty bags together. She put the two tins they had not used to one side and stretched out beside him. She didn't much care if she got grass stains on the new cotton skirt. Robert seemed uncaring, and she felt the same. The sun was warm on her eyelids, and the meal they had shared had made her drowsy. She didn't want to go to sleep, to miss any of this marvellous afternoon, but she couldn't help herself...

When she opened her eyes again, Robert was tickling her nose with a blade of grass. 'Do you realise it's almost half past six?' he asked humorously.

Sophie caught her breath. 'Half past six?' She pushed his teasing hand away. 'But the Pages are coming at seven o'clock, and your mother always likes to serve dinner by a quarter to eight!'

Robert nodded. 'I know.' But he didn't look perturbed.

'Well, we're going to be awfully late!'

'Awfully,' he agreed.

She stared up at him. 'Don't you care?'

'Not particularly.' He trailed the fingers of one hand down her cheek, her throat, the curve of her breast to her waist. His eyes had darkened perceptibly and there was a curious desperation in his voice as he said: 'How would you like to have dinner with me instead? There's an old country pub around here which serves the most delicious duckling you've ever tasted.'

'But, Robert, you told Sally . . .'

'That we couldn't dine with them? I know. Did you want to?' His voice had cooled slightly.

'You know I didn't,' she exclaimed, conscious of his fingers caressing the skin of her waist beneath the fine texture of her jersey. 'But what about your mother?'

Robert lowered his head to kiss the curve of her jaw-line. 'I don't want to spend the evening with my mother,' he murmured huskily, 'I want to spend it with you.'

'But, Robert——' Sophie was finding it incredibly difficult to maintain any sense of coherency in all this. 'Robert—on the way here——'

'On the way here I behaved as I should be behaving right now,' he conceded, biting the lobe of her ear. 'But this might be the last——' He broke off abruptly. 'Sophie, stop trying to find reasons for everything. Just kiss me—no—no, not like that. Like this . . .' And his mouth parted her lips and the hard strength of his body was pressing her back into the soft green turf.

Robert kissed her many times—long, drugging kisses that made her tremble with emotions she didn't alto-gether understand. She had the feeling that she was dreaming all this and that at the end there was going to be a rude awakening. He had never kissed her in quite this way before, and although she sensed that what they were doing was wrong, she didn't know why. He was caressing her in a deliberately arousing way that made her arch her back towards him and ache with unknown longings and desires. And then, when she had lost all sense of inhibition and was almost wantonly yielding and responsive in his arms, he drew himself forcibly away from her, sitting with his legs drawn up in a hunched position, his head resting on his knees.

It took Sophie some minutes to realise that had he not made the break when he did, he would not have been capable of doing so. She could have refused him nothing, and the fact that he had not taken her innocence was, to her, an example of the respect he had for her.

She sat up at last and scrambling on to her knees slid her arms over his shoulders and round his neck from behind. For a second he resisted and then he allowed her hands to slide down over the hair-roughened skin of his chest, holding him closely back against her. She rested her chin on his shoulder and said softly: 'I love you, Robert. I'm sorry, but I can't help it.'

Robert bent his head and put his lips to her bare arm. 'I'm sorry, too, Sophie,' he muttered thickly. 'Because I'm very much afraid I love you, too.'

Sophie slid round him to stare into his impassioned dark face. 'Oh, Robert,' she breathed unsteadily, 'don't be sorry.'

Robert put her gently but firmly away from him and got to his feet, brushing down his trousers. 'Come on,' he said, but there was no edge to his urgency. 'I think we need bright lights and music and people, don't you? This place is much too secluded, the way I feel at the moment.'

They had dinner at the small country inn Robert had designated. The tables were all booked for the evening, but he was apparently known there and presently a table for two was produced for them. The food was delicious, as he had decreed. They ate fresh salmon, duckling dripping with orange sauce, a chocolate dessert that was coated with nuts and raisins. They drank a dry white wine that tingled on the palate, and Sophie had never been so happy. The fact that her long cotton skirt and simple jersey were in contrast to most of the elegantly dressed women there made not the slightest difference to her when Robert devoured her with his eyes every time he looked across the table at her.

Actually, she had washed her face and hands and combed her hair in the cloakroom before joining him in the bar before the meal, and her honey-gold skin and thick silky mane required no additional adornment. She had attracted a number of men's eyes already, and Robert was not ignorant of the fact.

They lingered over their coffee, Robert enjoying a brandy with his, and then they emerged into the soft scented dusk and walked without haste to where they had left the car. Sophie felt ridiculously happy and sad all at the same time. Throughout the meal they had talked desultorily, but always about impersonal topics, and not once had they mentioned the thing which had to be uppermost in both their minds. She longed for him to give some further indication of his feelings for her; her own had never been in any doubt, and his earlier reluctance to admit his love for her was the only flaw in what had been a perfect evening.

In the car, he gave his attention to the lights and the ignition and Sophie fastened her safety belt with nervous fingers. Surely he would say something now that they were alone.

But he didn't. The journey home was accomplished almost in silence and although she managed to convince herself that it was a companionable silence, there was an essence of restraint about it.

The Pages' car was still standing in the drive at

Penn Warren and Robert uttered an irritated ejaculation. 'That's all I need!' he said harshly, standing on his brakes.

Sophie unfastened her safety strap. 'Well, thank you for a lovely evening anyway,' she was beginning jerkily, when his fingers curved around her neck, under the weight of her hair, dragging her closely against him.

'Don't thank me, Sophie,' he groaned passionately, burying his face in her hair. 'Dear God, I want to make love to you.' His breathing was erratic. 'I should never have begun this. I knew I wouldn't want to stop...'

His mouth was hungry and possessive, his breath sweet and scented with the brandy. Sophie's head swam, and her limbs ached to be closer to him than the gear consol would allow, and she was holding his face between her hands and covering it with kisses when the car door was suddenly wrenched open and a draught of cool air swept into the heated interior.

'You swine, Robert!' muttered Simon, glaring at them in the light of the powerful torch he held in his hands. 'You couldn't leave her alone, could you?'

Robert put Sophie away from him and got slowly out of the car. Sophie scrambled out, too, sure this was certain to erupt into a fight this time, and terrified for both of them.

'Simon, please——' she begged, grasping his arm, but he shook her off.

'Go inside, Sophie. This is between Rob and me.'

'No! No, it's not.' Sophie appealed to Robert as he came round the car. 'Robert—Robert, don't do anything you're liable to regret.'

Robert spared her an impatient glance and then he looked at his brother. 'You've been asking for this, Simon.'

'Have I?' Simon seemed determined to taunt him. 'And what have you been asking for, I wonder?' His lip curled. 'One woman isn't enough for you, is it? You have to take mine as well.'

Sophie put herself between them. 'I'm not your woman, Simon——' she exclaimed, but Simon ignored her.

'Anyway, as it happens, you don't have the time right now to settle any scores with anyone,' he went on bitterly. 'You've got company. Oh, not the Pages—although they're here as well, and avid to know where you and Sophie have been all evening. No, your fiancée is here, Robert—Emma! Don't you think you ought to go in and say hello to her before she, like me, begins to wonder what can be delaying you so long in the driveway?'

CHAPTER FIVE

Sophie had been sick, violently and nauseatingly sick, and her indisposition had served the dual purpose of ridding her body of the food which had gone sour on her, and giving her a vital excuse for not joining her parents and their guests downstairs.

After Simon's shattering announcement, it had taken Robert fully a minute to grasp what he was saying. Then he had turned, his face grim, and strode away towards the house leaving Sophie to stand shivering beside the car. She had been so shocked, her teeth had started to chatter, and Simon had taken pity on her and putting an arm about her had almost carried her to the house. He had helped her up the stairs and into her bedroom, and then the nausea which had been welling up inside her filled her mouth and she had had to run into the bathroom. She had stood there vomiting for almost five minutes and when she finally turned, Simon was leaning against the bathroom wall right behind her, holding out a soft towel for her to wipe her sweating face.

But now she was back in the bedroom, weak and trembling, but drained of the sick apprehension which had overwhelmed her. She fumbled unsteadily with the zip fastener of her skirt, and Simon, who was standing near the door regarding her anxiously, said: 'Are you sure you're all right now?'

Sophie nodded vigorously. 'Of—of course. It—it must have been something I'd eaten——'

'Don't tell me lies, Sophie, on top of everything else,' he exclaimed savagely. 'I know perfectly well what's wrong with you! You didn't know Robert was engaged, did you? He didn't tell you. The very reason your father sent him to meet you at the station when you first returned home—so he could advise you of that fact. But he conveniently forgot!'

Sophie's lips were dry. 'Simon, please . . .'

Simon's fists clenched and unclenched by his sides. 'I could kill him. I really could!'

'I'm tired, Simon . . .'

'My brother! My sainted brother! I always admired him, do you know that? Always looked up to him! But he's no better than an animal—a buck stag——'

'*Simon!*'

His mother's voice brought him up short, and he glanced round, flushing as his mother came into the room. She took in Sophie's distressed appearance in a moment and then turned back to her son.

'Go downstairs, Simon,' she advised him coldly. 'Vicky is waiting to say goodbye to you.'

Simon looked as though he was about to argue, but something in Sophie's pale exhausted face caused him to change his mind. Without a word he turned and left them, slamming the door behind him. Then Laura approached her stepdaughter, pushing Sophie's hands aside and unloosening the skirt fastener for her. When the girl had stepped out of it, Laura picked it up and threw it over a chair, and then helped her off with her jersey. When the folds of her cotton nightdress had been slipped over her head, Sophie pulled back the bedcovers and slipped between the sheets. Then she stared miserably up at her stepmother, waiting for the axe to fall.

But Laura merely shook her head resignedly and said: 'How do you feel now, Sophie?'

'I'm all right.' Sophie's voice was muffled.

'Are you?' Laura stood looking down at her. 'Oh, my

dear, we didn't want you to be hurt.'

Sophie closed her eyes. Open, they were too revealing. 'Hurt?' she echoed quickly. 'I don't know what you mean.'

'Yes, you do. Sophie, I couldn't help overhearing what Simon was saying as I came along the landing. Robert didn't tell you, did he? I should have guessed he hadn't. You were too—happy with him to have known. Going out with him this afternoon.' She shook her head. 'I should have listened to your father. I should have stopped you. I know he didn't approve. But we believed you knew...' She broke off. 'Well, you might as well know it all. Emma's here for a few days' holiday. Robert will be returning to Cymtraeth next week, but Emma will be staying on. They're planning to get married later in the year.'

Sophie thought she could not feel any more pain, but she could—hot searing pain that caused a sob of pure agony to escape her. Uncaring of what Laura must be thinking of her, she rolled over on to her stomach and buried her face in the pillow, sobbing uncontrollably.

'Oh, Sophie!' Laura sat down beside her on the bed. She put a hand on the girl's heaving shoulders. 'Sophie, don't take it so badly. It had to happen sooner or later. You must have known that! One day he was bound to find the right girl—the woman he could love——'

'He doesn't love her,' choked Sophie. 'He loves me——'

'I know he loves you, darling. You're his little sister. Both the boys love you——'

'No—no!' Sophie twisted her head from side to side. 'Not like that. He loves me—he really loves me!'

'Stop it, Sophie!' Laura was beginning to sound a little impatient now. 'You mustn't lose control of yourself like this. It's not good for you, and how do you think Emma would feel if she could hear you——'

'I don't care about Emma!'

'Well, that's not very kind, is it? Sophie, Sophie—Emma is going to be your sister-in-law. You should be happy for her—for both of them. I think they'll be very happy together. And think how nice it will be to have a sister——'

Sophie's only response was to drag a pillow over her head to shut out the sound of her stepmother's voice, and with an exclamation Laura got to her feet.

'I think you're being very silly, Sophie,' she said reprovingly. 'I've tried to be patient with you, to understand you, but I can't condone such selfish behaviour. I think I'd better leave you to pull yourself together. We'll talk about this later.' She paused. 'But I would —beg you not to say anything to Emma about this. I don't want her upset, and I shall be very angry if you try to cause trouble between her and Robert.'

Sophie didn't answer, and with a heavy sigh her stepmother walked to the bedroom door. She opened it and then gasped: 'Robert! What are you doing here?'

Sophie stopped sobbing and listened.

'I came to find you, Mother. The Pages are leaving.' He looked beyond her into the bedroom. 'Where's Sophie?'

Laura tried to block his view of the bed with her body, but Sophie thrust the pillows aside and lifted a ravaged face to look at him.

'My God! Sophie!' he muttered, and would have pushed his mother aside and entered the room had she not lifted a hand and struck him hard across his face. It was the first time she had laid a hand on him since he was a schoolboy.

'Don't you dare to go near her!' she commanded fiercely. 'Haven't you done enough?'

Robert stared at his mother disbelievingly, raising a hand to touch the stinging marks left by her fingers. Then his expression hardened. 'What's the matter with Sophie?' he demanded.

Laura was holding herself taut, but Sophie could sense the effort it was costing her. 'She's got a headache,' she replied evenly. 'A—sick headache.'

'I want to speak to her,' said Robert in controlled tones.

'You can't——' Laura's hands curled into her palms. 'Robert—please——'

Sophie couldn't bear the agonised appeal in her stepmother's voice. With a tremulous intake of breath, she buried her face under the covers, pulling the pillow back over her head.

'Sophie!' Robert's voice came across to her, but she didn't look up again. 'Sophie—speak to me!'

'Go away,' she moaned from beneath her pillows. 'Just go away. I don't want to speak to—to anyone.'

She heard her bedroom door close a few moments later and tentatively lifted her head, half expecting her stepmother to be in the room with her. But she was alone.

Sophie slept the sleep of exhaustion and awakened in the early morning when the first faint fingers of sunlight were probing the curtains at her windows. She awoke with an aching head and a horrible taste in her mouth, and she slid out of bed and padded into the bathroom to get a drink and two aspirins. For a few minutes she was able to keep her thoughts at bay, but as her conscious mind took full possession they came flooding back to torment her. The events of the evening before filled her with trepidation, and she sat down on the edge of the bed, burying her face in her hands.

No wonder Robert had been so reluctant to tell her he loved her. She doubted in the cold light of morning that he really did. Perhaps he had only told her that because she had said she loved him. Perhaps he had felt guilty...

She lifted her head and stared without pleasure at her reflection mirrored in the vanity unit. She looked terrible. Not even a night's sleep had been sufficient to erase the puffiness from her eyelids, and her pallor was pronounced and unhealthy-looking. Dear God, she thought painfully; what must Robert have thought when he saw her like this?

She dreaded the thought of the day ahead. She dreaded the idea of meeting Emma again. To imagine her and Robert together conjured up the kind of pictures in her mind that lacerated her soul. Did he love Emma? Or had he some other reason for marrying her? But what other reason could there be? She wasn't rich or of influential parentage, like some of the girls he had escorted in past years. She was attractive, but Robert knew dozens of attractive girls. Sophie shook her head. How on earth was she to go on as though nothing momentous had happened? Was that what Robert expected her to do? Or had his reasons for coming to her room last night been of a more personal nature? Might he be considering breaking off his engagement?

So many thoughts, so many unanswered questions. She would make herself ill if she continued to plague her brain like this. Already her headache felt worse, and the aspirins seemed to have had little effect.

Getting up, she went back into the bathroom and took a cold shower. The spray of water was like icy needles against her hot skin and her whole body tingled when it was over. But she did feel quite a bit better, and she quickly dressed in her shirt and jeans while the energy to do so possessed her. She brushed her hair and pinched her cheeks to give them a trace of colour, and was almost satisfied with the result. She no longer looked half dead.

It was only a few minutes after seven when she went downstairs. No one else was about, and she plugged in the kettle and carried the newspapers into the lounge. The room smelt of stale spirits and cigarette smoke, and she pulled back the curtains, thrusting open the windows. The air was cool and fresh and she took several deep breaths to clear her lungs. Then she settled down on the couch with the papers to wait for the kettle to boil, forcing herself to concentrate on the news of the day.

The headlines spoke of a rebellion in some South American republic; there was a threatened strike in the car industry, and some well-known politician had been served with a paternity suit. With a grimace Sophie turned to the inner pages, to the local news, trying to feel enthusiasm that the Conwynneth Young Farmers' Group Social had made almost two hundred pounds for charity. She had been to one of their socials, with Simon, but that had been almost two years ago now.

An article that did interest her concerned a local historian who was presently engaged in writing another book on Greek mythology. Sophie had always enjoyed reading the Greek legends at school, and in fact she had taken Greek at ordinary level and passed without difficulty. Languages had come easily to her and years ago she had contemplated becoming an interpreter.

The kettle began to whistle and she thrust down the papers and hurried into the kitchen. She made the tea and then set a tray for her parents, adding the plate of biscuits she knew her father enjoyed. She considered taking tea up to Robert and Simon and then dismissed the thought. If she did that, she would have to take one to Emma, too, and she had no desire to encounter the older girl earlier than was necessary.

Laura was awake when she knocked at her parents' bedroom door and tentatively went in. She was lying on her back staring blankly up at the ceiling, but when she saw Sophie a certain amount of relief spread over her drawn features.

'Good morning,' whispered Sophie, reassured that her father seemed to be sleeping peacefully. 'Where shall I put this?'

'Over here.' Laura sat up and cleared a space on the table at her side of the double bed. Then as Sophie set down the tray: 'How—how are you this morning, Sophie?'

Sophie straightened. 'Oh, I'm fine.' She pressed her lips together. 'Is that convenient for you?'

'Yes, of course.' Laura barely glanced at the tray. 'Sophie, I'm sorry—about what happened——'

'It's all right—really.' Sophie backed away. The last thing she wanted was to talk about that now. 'Well, I'll see you later,' and she quickly got through the door and closed it securely behind her.

On the landing she hesitated. Robert's door was only a few yards away. Ought she to go and speak to him now—ask him exactly what his intentions were? The desire to have the situation made known to her was an irresistible compulsion.

She stepped lightly across the carpet and turned the handle of his door. It gave easily, opening into the darkened room. But Robert's bed was empty. It hadn't even been slept in.

Sophie stepped outside again, forcing her fingers not to fumble over the handle. Her eyes darted to the door of the spare room where Emma was sleeping and all the familiar sickness from last night welled up inside her again. Oh, God, she thought, stumbling towards the stairs. He must have spent the night in Emma's bed...

Downstairs, her tea was growing cold. She picked up her cup and held it to her trembling lips. How could he, she thought desperately, *how could he*?

She was so wrapped up in her own misery that she was scarcely conscious of anyone approaching up the garden path until the back door opened behind her. She swung round almost spilling her tea, and caught her breath as Robert came into the kitchen. His eyes flickered over her broodingly and then he said: 'I'm sorry if I startled you. I didn't expect anyone to be about yet.'

Sophie's cup rattled into its saucer. 'Wh—where have you been?' He was still wearing the grey suit from the night before, and there was a dark growth of stubble on his chin.

Robert didn't immediately answer her. He walked over to the teapot and reaching down a cup poured himself some. He added milk and sugar and drank half of it before saying: 'I've been walking.' He drained the cup and poured another. 'How about you?'

Sophie made a helpless gesture. 'I—I just got up.'

'Did you sleep well?'

'Did you?'

Robert shook his head, looking down at his cup. 'I didn't go to bed.'

'*Robert!*'

He sighed heavily. 'Your father and I were talking until about four, and then I couldn't stand the atmosphere in here. I had to get out. I walked to High Apsdale.'

Sophie was aghast. 'But that's five miles!'

'I'm aware of that.' Robert ran a hand over his rough chin. 'God, I'm a mess! I need a shave.'

'You must be exhausted,' she exclaimed, as awareness of the unfairness of her earlier thoughts brought a rush of guilty colour to her cheeks. 'What—what were you and Daddy talking about?'

Robert pulled off his tie. 'This and that,' he replied uncompromisingly.

Sophie twisted her hands together. 'Me?'

He swallowed the remains of his second cup of tea. 'Among other things.' He stretched his shoulders wearily. 'And now, if you'll excuse me, I don't have a lot of time. I need a shower and a change of clothes before leaving.'

'*Leaving?*' Sophie stared at him aghast. 'But—but you can't be leaving!'

'Can't I?' Robert looked at her steadily.

Sophie took a gulp of air, and turned her back on him. 'You—you don't have to, you know,' she got out jerkily. 'I mean—I know I made a fool of myself last night, but it won't happen again, I—I can assure you. And your mother was upset...' She paused. 'Don't leave on my account. I shan't embarrass you.'

There was a moment's silence, broken only by the ragged sound of her breathing, and then Robert brushed past her to reach the door into the hall. 'Don't be a fool, Sophie!' he muttered savagely, and slammed out of the room.

After he had left her, Sophie stood for several minutes staring at the panels of the door, and then she turned rather jerkily and looked round the kitchen. What had he meant? Why was he leaving? And what about his—fiancée?

She felt confused and disorientated. Surely there had not been some terrible row last night after she had succumbed to exhaustion. Her father couldn't have asked him to leave, could he? Was that why Laura was awake? Hadn't she been to sleep—because Sophie had no doubt that if her father and Robert had been up till four a.m. Laura had been up, too.

She paced the floor restlessly. What ought she to do? Did Laura know her son was leaving, or had he come to this decision on his walk to High Apsdale? Where was he going? And when? Before or after breakfast? She wished there was someone she could ask, but right now she felt herself to be the bone of contention between Robert and their parents, and there was no one she could turn to.

But at least this new development had served to banish some of the self-depression which had filled her. It would come back, but at the moment Robert's intentions troubled her more. She didn't want to be responsible for destroying the good relationship he had always had with her father, and nor did she want to feel that through her Laura was estranged from her son.

What could she do? She had tried apologising to Robert and that had served no purpose except perhaps to make him impatient with her. If she appealed to him to stay for his mother's sake, might he listen to her? She doubted it. There had been something hard and determined about his set face, and in her vulnerable mental state she was disinclined to trust her own abilities.

She was standing, undecided, in the middle of the floor when her stepmother entered the kitchen. Unlike Sophie, she was not dressed, but she was carrying the tray Sophie had taken up earlier.

'Your father's still asleep,' she explained tiredly, indicating the unused cup and saucer. 'I'd rather not wake him yet.' Sophie nodded and she went on: 'I've just spoken to Robert. He says he's leaving.'

'Yes,' Sophie nodded again. 'He—he came in just now. He's been—walking.'

'Yes, I know.' Laura set the tray down heavily. 'Is there any more tea? I could do with another cup.'

'Of course.' Sophie was glad of the task to occupy her hands. 'There you are.'

'Thank you.' Laura took the cup and sank down wearily on to one of the stools beside the breakfast bar. 'I'll have this and then I'll make some breakfast. Are you hungry?'

'Me?' Sophie shook her head. 'No.'

Laura bent to her cup. 'Nor am I.' She looked up. 'Does Robert want any breakfast?'

Sophie moved her shoulders helplessly. 'I don't know. I didn't ask.' She bit her lower lip. 'Where is he going?'

Laura sighed deeply. 'He's going to his apartment in London over the weekend, and then to Cymtraeth on Monday morning.'

'But why?' Sophie burst out. 'I thought—that is——' She sought for words. 'Emma's here!'

'I'm sure he's aware of that.' Laura's tone was dry. Then she shook her head in a confused way. 'Who knows what Robert is thinking? My God, I never thought it would come to this!'

'To what? What would come to this?' Sophie stared at her desperately. 'Mummy, what happened last night?'

Laura finished her tea and pushed her cup aside. 'Nothing that need concern you, Sophie,' she replied flatly. 'I've no doubt everything will turn out for the best. So far as Emma is concerned, Robert has to return to the site a couple of days earlier than he'd planned, do you understand?'

Sophie's facial muscles stiffened. She understood. She understood that so far as Laura was concerned appearances must be maintained at all costs, and whatever Robert's reasons for leaving the *status quo* would be maintained.

But what did Robert think about it? What was behind his sudden departure for London? Then her shoulders sagged. Did it matter? Really? If Robert had had anything to tell her, he had had ample opportunity a few minutes ago, and the fact that he hadn't pointed to a dwindling of interest on his part. It seemed apparent that there had been some kind of argument last night and Robert was leaving to avoid the aftermath. But no doubt in a couple of weeks it would all blow over and things would go on as they had before, with the wedding looming larger on the horizon every day.

Laura was taking ham and eggs out of the fridge and turning on the grill. The smell of the uncooked food sickened Sophie, and with a brief word of explanation she left the kitchen. She felt lost and desperate, a feeling which was in no way dispelled when Robert came running down the stairs, showered and changed into mud-coloured levis and a cream knitted shirt. Drops of water still sparkled on his dark hair, and although there were lines etched about his eyes and beside his mouth, he exuded an aura of male strength and superiority.

When he saw Sophie hovering in the hall, he said harshly: 'Where's my mother?'

'In the kitchen.' Sophie wiped her moist palms over the seat of her jeans. 'Robert—Robert, why are you leaving?' She drew a deep breath. 'I—please—don't go on my account.'

Robert halted in front of her, looking down at her with eyes darkened almost to blackness by the shadows of the panelled hall. 'Stop feeling so sorry for yourself!' he advised her roughly. 'I have—things to do in

London, that's all.'

Sophie thrust her trembling hands into the waistband of the jeans. 'And—and yesterday?' she managed, with great temerity.

Robert sighed. 'I think you'd better try and forget about yesterday,' he told her heavily.

Sophie felt frozen inside. Until then she had foolishly harboured some hopes that Robert was leaving because he could no longer face his fiancée knowing he was in love with another woman. Now, hearing him tell her to try and forget those moments by the stream —that intimate dinner for two—their subsequent lovemaking in the car—was comparable to having him produce a knife and insert it between her ribs and turn the blade with slow precision.

Something of her horror must have shown in her face, for he said violently: 'Don't look at me like that, Sophie, for God's sake! It's for your own good! You're wasting your time with me!'

And with a muffled oath, he pushed past her and entered the kitchen.

CHAPTER SIX

THE only person who seemed to have slept well the night before was Emma. She came downstairs almost two hours after the Jensen had roared away to London, apparently innocent of any undercurrents in the atmosphere.

Sophie and her stepmother were sitting in the kitchen, sharing a pot of coffee and deliberately avoiding any discussion of personal issues, when Emma poked her head shyly round the door, apologising for interrupting them. 'I'm awfully sorry, Mrs. Kemble,' she went on. 'I'm afraid I overslept. Your beds are so comfortable!'

'That's all right, Emma. Come in.'

Laura glanced awkwardly at her stepdaughter as Emma entered the kitchen, and Sophie encountered that troubled gaze. Then she looked at Emma. Emma hadn't changed. Her manner still jarred on Sophie. Her unassuming shyness, Sophie found coy, and the nervous smile seemed false. Emma was dressed in a simple belted cotton dress, her dark hair framed her small face in bobbing curls, and Sophie thought uncharitably that she was exactly the kind of girl any mother would find it hard to object to. Only Sophie saw the calculation behind the pose. Or did she? She stared miserably down into her coffee cup. How could she be expected to view Emma with anything but jealousy and mistrust?

'Hello, Sophie,' Emma was saying now, as Laura moved to make some fresh coffee. 'I'm sorry you were ill last evening. Are you better now?'

Sophie looked up, schooling her features. 'Hello, Emma,' she responded tautly. 'Yes, I'm much better, thank you.'

Emma sat down beside her. 'It must have been something you ate,' she commented, looking happily round the kitchen. 'Hmm, this is a lovely room, isn't it? So cosy! I love old houses, don't you? They have so much more character than modern ones, don't you think?'

Sophie made some non-committal reply, and Emma went on: 'I was just saying to Robbie——' Sophie inwardly cringed. Only Emma had ever called Robert 'Robbie'; '——I was just saying the last time he was in town that when we're married we must buy a cottage in the country for weekends, Mrs. Kemble. Perhaps we could find something here—in Conwynneth. That would be nice, wouldn't it? With me not having any parents of my own, I do appreciate feeling myself part of a family again.'

Laura gave her stepdaughter a second glance. Then she returned her attention to Emma. 'Well—er—we love having you, Emma...'

Emma rested her elbows on the breakfast bar. 'Where is Robbie, anyway? Surely he hasn't overslept, too? I didn't look into his bedroom. I could hear somebody snoring and I didn't want to disturb him——'

'That would be my husband,' said Laura quietly, pushing the coffee jug towards her. 'Do help yourself. As—er—as a matter of fact, Robert isn't here.'

Emma paused in the process of pouring steaming coffee into her cup. 'He's not here?' she echoed disbelievingly.

'No. No, not here.' Laura forced a smile. 'He—er—there was some sort of emergency at the site. He had to go back a couple of days earlier than expected and as you were asleep...' Her voice trailed away.

'I see.' Emma finished pouring her coffee and Sophie noticed that her hand was quite steady as she did so. Hardly the reaction of a somewhat shy and nervous person. 'Did he say if he'd be back?'

Laura shook her head and busied herself collecting hers and Sophie's dirty cups. 'I don't think he'll get back while you're here, my dear. But that makes no difference. We'll try to make sure that you enjoy your little holiday.'

Emma looked up and smiled. 'I'm sure you will, Mrs. Kemble. And I always enjoy myself here, you know that. Naturally, I'm disappointed that Robbie's had to leave——' Her gaze flicked fleetingly towards Sophie, and then back to the older woman again. 'But it's not as though we haven't seen much of one another lately. I mean, since he's been staying here we've seen quite a lot of each other.'

Sophie's fingers curled into her palms. So that was where Robert had spent his days. In London. An awful sense of desolation filled her.

'Of course.' Laura was speaking now. 'I knew you'd understand, Emma. You're such an—undemanding girl.'

Sophie couldn't stand much more of this. She got to her feet and thrust her thumbs into the low belt of her jeans. 'I think I'll go for a walk,' she remarked with enforced nonchalance. 'It's such a lovely morning...'

'If you wait a few minutes, I'll come with you,' exclaimed Emma at once, gulping her coffee. 'I'd love a walk.'

Sophie and Laura exchanged glances, Sophie's aggressive, Laura's appealing. Sophie gave in. 'All right,' she agreed briefly. 'I'll be in the garden.'

The air outside was infinitely refreshing after the tenseness of the atmosphere in the kitchen. Sophie walked slowly over the lawns, her shoulders hunched, desperately seeking composure.

'Sophie! Hi, Sophie!'

She turned at the sound of her name on masculine lips. The boy hurrying towards her across the grass was lanky tall and fair, dressed in cream tee-shirt and shorts. He was carrying a tennis racket, and with a sense of resignation she recognised him as the boy her stepmother had mentioned had been asking for her.

He reached her side and looked down at her admiringly. 'Hi, Sophie. Remember me?'

Sophie forced a smile. 'Yes, of course. Hello, Graham.'

Graham nodded, obviously relieved. 'I came to see whether you had time for a game,' he went on, indicating his racket. 'Actually, I was going to come last weekend, but I've had the most ghastly cold. I'm only just beginning to feel normal again.'

Sophie gave a sympathetic shake of her head. 'Bad luck!'

'Yes, wasn't it? Summer colds are the hardest to shed, so I'm told. Anyway, I'm here now. How about it?'

'I can't.' Sophie hesitated. 'I've promised to go for a walk with—with Emma. Do you know Emma?'

'Actually, no. She's Robert's fiancée, isn't she? I've heard of her, of course. My sister's engaged to John Meredith and——'

'I know.' Sophie didn't want to hear all that again. 'They all go out together.' She broke off and looked towards the house. 'Well, here she comes now. I'll introduce you.'

And as she did so, an idea occurred to her.

'As Graham is here,' she suggested, 'why don't we play tennis instead?' It would avoid the unwanted *tête-à-tête* with Emma. 'You and I could play, Emma, and then Graham could play the winner. Just one set each, of course.'

Emma looked doubtful. 'I don't play tennis awfully well,' she demurred, with her coy smile.

'Nor do I,' lied Sophie, her fingers crossed behind her back, and set out to prove that Emma could beat her without any difficulty.

The soft court behind the house had seen dozens of games between Sophie and her stepbrothers. They had always been needle matches with Sophie striving for every point. Never had the court witnessed her playing so deliberately badly as she did that morning. If Graham suspected her subterfuge, there was nothing he could do about it, and when she disappeared during his set with Emma the message she wanted to convey was not too hard to grasp.

Sophie had made her way up to her room. She was in no mood to be sociable to anyone, and the prospect of the weeks ahead had never seemed so bleak.

During the next few days, Sophie managed to evade any confidential conversations with Emma. It wasn't too difficult. She was still helping her father in the mornings, and Laura roped Simon in to entertain their guest. Consequently Sophie had plenty of time to think about and brood over her future.

In the middle of the week Simon cornered her alone in the dining room as she was setting the table for lunch and said bitterly: 'Are you avoiding me, Sophie?'

'Avoiding you, Simon? Don't be silly!'

He came round the table, blocking her exit. 'I never seem to see you alone these days.'

'You've been—entertaining—Emma.' Sophie was flushed.

'Keeping her out of the way, don't you mean?' Simon thrust his hands aggressively into the pockets of his cotton pants. 'Oh, Sophie! Are you furious with me?'

Sophie concentrated on setting out the knives and forks. 'You're talking nonsense, and you know it.' She straightened. 'Will you get out of my way? I want to finish.'

Simon remained where he was. 'You are angry with me, aren't you? Why? Because I told you the truth about Rob? Didn't you want to know, was that it?'

Sophie looked down at the cloth. 'I'd rather not talk about it, if you don't mind.'

'Sooner or later you've got to.'

'Do I?' Sophie heaved a sigh. 'Simon, please! Your mother is waiting to serve the lunch.'

'To hell with the lunch!' Simon's face was grim. 'Sophie,' he appealed again. 'Sophie, what do you want me to say and I'll say it?'

Sophie looked up at him helplessly. Then she put her hand on his arm. 'Simon, I——'

'Oh, so there you are, Simon!' Emma's somewhat shrill tones interrupted them, and Simon smothered an oath as he turned to face her. Emma came lightly across the coffee and cream-flecked carpet. 'I've been looking everywhere for you, Simon. Look, here are the snaps I was telling you about.'

Sophie turned back to the table as Simon moved away to examine the photographs Emma was holding out to him. She finished setting the table and would have left the room had Emma not called her back:

'Come and see, Sophie. These are some snaps Robbie and I took in Portugal in April. Aren't they good?'

Sophie's nerves stretched. Robert had been working in Portugal from February through to May. She hadn't known that any of his girl-friends ever visited him on a job. But then Emma wasn't just *any* girl-friend, was she?

It tore Sophie's emotions anew to see pictures of Robert taken in the Moorish quarter of Lisbon, dancing with Emma at a nightclub, relaxing on the beach at Estoril, lean and tanned in narrow bathing trunks.

'Very nice,' she managed tautly, and ignoring Simon's instinctive sympathy she left them.

However, in the late afternoon, when she was lying on her bed trying to make sense of the historical novel in front of her, her bedroom door opened and her younger stepbrother entered the room. She jack-knifed into a sitting position and regarded him with a hostile expression. 'Yes?'

Simon closed the door and leaned back against it. 'What are you doing up here? It's a glorious afternoon.'

'Then why aren't you out in it?' she countered shortly.

Simon sighed. 'I came to find you. Did you know that there's a dance at the village hall tonight? It should be quite a decent affair. They've brought some group in from Liverpool, and there's to be refreshments. Would you like to go?'

'No, thank you.'

'Sophie!'

'Well, I don't want to.'

'Why not?'

'I don't feel like dancing.' She paused. 'You go. Take Emma. I'm sure she'd be only too pleased——'

'Stop being bitchy! Emma is going, as a matter of fact. John Meredith and his fiancée are going and they've invited her to go with them.'

'Hard luck!'

Simon moved away from the door. 'Sophie, stop being so sarcastic! You know perfectly well that I have no interest in Emma. That's Rob's prerogative.'

Sophie winced at the intended barb and Simon looked instantly contrite. 'You make me say these

99

things, Sophie,' he exclaimed. 'Please—I'm asking you. Come to the dance with me.'

Sophie looked down at the bed coverlet. 'Ask Vicky,' she replied gruffly.

'I don't want to ask Vicky.' Simon raised his eyes heavenward. 'What is it you want of me, Sophie? Would you like me to make love to you—to demonstrate that I have feelings, too? Is that what you need?'

Sophie lifted her head reluctantly. It wasn't fair to make Simon a whipping-boy for her own frustration. 'No. No, of course not,' she managed, in a small voice. 'I'm sorry, Simon. If—if you really want to take me to the dance, then—then all right, I'll come.'

Simon's eyes darkened as he looked down at her. 'Oh, Sophie,' he muttered huskily, and then he came down beside her on the bed, leaning forward and putting his lips to hers.

It was the first time he had kissed her since they were children, and although Sophie did not find the touch of his lips repulsive to her, nor did she feel anything more than an immense compassion for him. She allowed him to be the one to draw back, and when he did, she said:

'I think you'd better go now, Simon. I'd hate to think what your mother would say if she found you here—like this.'

'I don't care what she'd say,' he muttered fiercely, and would have kissed her again, but now Sophie drew back.

'Well, I do,' she insisted gently. 'What time do we have to leave tonight?'

Simon paused near the door. 'John and Joanna are calling for Emma about eight. I guess we could leave then, too.'

'Fine.'

Sophie smiled, and reassured, Simon left her. But

100

after he had gone Sophie wondered whether, in the circumstances, she should have stuck to her refusal. It wasn't fair to allow Simon to think that she could ever care for him in that way.

Sophie delayed coming downstairs until she was sure Emma had departed. A trip to Hereford with her step-mother and Emma earlier in the week had yielded two long dresses suitable for either day or evening wear, and although at the time her initial impulse had been to refuse Laura's generous offer, she was glad now she had not given in to the impulse. She had chosen to wear the one with the low round neckline and long sleeves. It was very plain below a high bustline, and made of the kind of material that clung where it touched and was patterned in shades of green and grey. She knew it suited her. She knew it enhanced the honey-gold tan she had acquired, and she also knew that her appearance would in some part reassure her parents that she had recovered from her malaise. If they had equal doubts as to the advisability of allow-ing her to go out with Simon, they were prepared to overlook them for the present.

Simon's reaction to her appearance was very flatter-ing, and although she knew that that part of her which responded to his attentions was remote from the in-tegral functions of her body which Robert had devas-tated, she nevertheless enjoyed the feeling of being ad-mired after the shattering experiences of last weekend.

By the time they arrived at the hall and found somewhere to park Simon's station wagon, the dance was already well under way. Village affairs tended to be supervised by the clergy and consequently midnight was considered quite late enough to close the hall. This meant that the young people arrived earlier in-stead of imbibing liberally at the Bay Horse first.

The hall was large and spacious, festooned with streamers and balloons. The group was already playing on the stage at one end of the hall, while at the other buffet tables provided an assortment of refreshments. And in spite of Sophie's misgivings, she and Simon were inevitably engulfed by the crowd that included John Meredith and his fiancée and Emma. Still, they were dancing most of the time, and in the throng of young people it was possible to lose oneself completely. Emma seemed to be enjoying herself, too. Several of the boys had asked her to dance and only Simon hung back, monopolising Sophie.

But eventually John Meredith insinuated himself between them and asked Sophie to dance with him. Simon turned to ask Joanna, but she was already dancing with someone else and only Emma was available. Sophie met his frustrated glare as she followed John out on to the floor and felt guiltily aware that she could have refused and remained with him. However, after a few minutes she forgot Simon's problems as she encountered some problems of her own.

The group had disbanded for a break and the music now issuing from the loudspeakers came from records. Instead of the previous heavy beat music, the vicar had taken the opportunity to put on some soothing dance music, and the dreamy quality of the waltz caused John to draw her closely into his arms and lay his cheek against hers.

'This is better, isn't it?' he murmured, in her ear, and she was conscious of his lips moving in her hair.

'I think you should behave yourself, Mr. Meredith,' she answered coolly. 'I'd hate your fiancée to think I was encouraging you.'

John chuckled. 'Oh, you're so romantic, Miss Kemble,' he teased, and she smelt the aroma of whisky on his breath.

'And you've had too much to drink,' she countered, drawing back to look at him.

'I haven't.' His eyes mocked her. 'On my honour, I haven't had more than two drinks this evening.'

'Two drinks?' Sophie tipped her head on one side. 'But how big were they?'

John smiled. 'Ah, that would be telling!'

Conscious of his eyes appraising her appearance, Sophie glanced nervously about her. 'There are quite a lot of people here, aren't there? These affairs are very well patronised.'

'Are they?' John looked down at her dress. 'Did that possessive stepbrother of yours tell you how delicious you look?'

Sophie couldn't prevent a small smile. 'Not in those words, no.'

'I thought not. Well, I'm telling you. You look beautiful.' His expression sobered. 'Will you have dinner with me tomorrow evening?'

Sophie gasped, 'Of course not!'

'Why not?'

Sophie felt sure everyone could hear what he was saying even though the din of the music made it impossible. 'Because I can't.'

'Because of Joanna?'

Sophie looked down at the buttons on his jacket. What price now her vain boast to Robert that if John asked her out with him again she would go? But that had been before she had found out ... She pressed her lips tightly together. Before Robert had made such a fool of her!

'Well?' John squeezed her fingers within his own. 'Is it because of Joanna?'

'It should be.'

'Then it isn't just that?'

'Oh, John!' She looked up at him impatiently. 'Why

are you asking me to have dinner with you? You know very well that—that your loyalty is due to your fiancée.'

'What an old-fashioned expression!'

'Nevertheless, it's true.'

'All right, so it's true. That's my problem. But I would still like to take you out for dinner tomorrow evening.'

Sophie shook her head. 'I'm sorry.'

'Are you afraid of what your parents might say?' He paused. 'Or are you afraid of what—Robert will say?'

'What do you mean?'

'Oh, don't give me that, Sophie. Everyone knows how you feel about Robert—or rather, how you *think* you feel.'

Sophie swallowed hard and stared at him. 'I don't know what you mean.'

John sighed. 'Don't make me say it, Sophie.'

'Say it? Say what?'

'Sophie, everyone knows you've had a crush on Robert for years. Good lord, your parents knew about it, didn't they? As soon as that became apparent, you were packed off to boarding school.'

Sophie's cheeks burned. 'I see,' she managed tautly, while inside she was a seething mass of chaotic thoughts and emotions. 'Thank you for telling me.'

'Oh, come on, Sophie.' John uttered an exclamation, half ashamed of his outburst. 'It wasn't evident to everyone. Only Rob and I are the same age. I saw what the onlooker always sees.'

'And did you discuss this with him?' she asked tightly, aware of a rising sense of resentment against Robert for not telling her.

John coloured now. 'Hell, no! You should know Robert better than that.' He glanced round. 'Come on, let's go and get a drink. Oh——' as she would have

104

protested '—Coke, of course.'

Sophie acquiesced and they made their way to the end of the room. Cans of Coke and other soft drinks were pyramided on the end buffet table, and John paid for two and handed one to Sophie. 'We'll drink it in the corridor,' he said, making for the door so that she had, perforce, to follow him. 'It's too hot in here.'

It was infinitely cooler in the corridor, but Sophie felt momentarily doubtful about leaving the hall with John. Then she relaxed as indignation over what he had just told her hardened her scruples. At least no one should accuse her of having a crush on John; the running was all on his side; and if Joanna didn't like it, then perhaps she should find some more adequate way to control her errant fiancé.

'Now what are you thinking about?' John stretched out a hand and touched her forehead where a frown was drawing her dark brows together. 'You're not still mad at me for what I said just now, are you?'

Sophie swallowed a mouthful of Coke before replying. Then she shook her head. 'No. I was thinking about Joanna, as a matter of fact.'

John sighed and leaned back against the wall. 'What about Joanna?'

'Do you love her?'

'What's that got to do with anything?'

'Do you?'

John shrugged. 'I guess so.'

'Then why do you want to go out with me?'

John made an indifferent gesture. 'Loving Joanna doesn't blind me to the charms of other women.'

Sophie's lips tilted. 'Thank you.'

'For what?'

'Calling me a woman. It's the first time anyone's ever done that.'

John grinned. 'But not the last. Oh, Sophie, you will

have dinner with me, won't you?' he appealed.

Sophie hesitated. 'I'll think about it.'

'I'll pick you up at seven-thirty tomorrow evening,' stated John firmly.

'My parents will know,' she warned.

John made a face at her. 'Tough!'

Sophie gave him an exasperated stare. 'You must feel very sure of Joanna.'

'I do.' He narrowed his eyes. 'Not so sure of you, though, Sophie. You wouldn't let me down, would you?'

Sophie raised her eyebrows. 'You'll just have to wait to find out.'

The sound of voices and movement near the doors to the hall attracted their attention, and turning Sophie saw Simon and Joanna and several more of their crowd emerging, obviously looking for them.

'John!' As soon as she saw him, Joanna came towards her fiancé. 'What are you doing out here?' She cast an impatient look at Sophie. 'I thought you two were dancing.'

'We were.' John straightened away from the wall while Sophie countered Simon's unfriendly stare. 'But we were hot and thirsty. There's no law against drinking too many Cokes, is there?'

Joanna made a gallant effort to control her annoyance. 'No. No, of course not.' She forced herself to look at Sophie again. 'Are you all right? My inebriated fiancé hasn't been making a pass at you, I hope.'

Sophie bit her tongue. Then she too managed a sardonic smile. 'Oh, no. As a matter of fact we were talking about you, Joanna.' And with an encompassing look at all of them, she walked confidently back into the hall.

Simon caught up with her just inside the door. His fingers gripped her arm tightly and his face was grim and constrained. 'Just what the hell do you think you're playing at?' he demanded, in a low tone.

Sophie refused to look at him, allowing her eyes to range over the heads of the people nearest to them. 'I don't know what you mean.'

'Yes, you do. Going outside with John. How do you think Joanna felt when she found you had both disappeared?'

Sophie focused on him. 'I really don't care.'

Simon's jaw was taut. 'What's the matter with you?'

'Perhaps I'm trying to get my own back.'

Simon raised his eyes heavenward. 'You're not making sense.'

'Am I not?' Sophie tilted her head. 'I suppose you knew all about me being packed off to boarding school, didn't you? And the reasons behind it?'

Simon stared at her incredulously. 'What do you mean?'

'I've just explained. You knew why they did it, don't you? You were taken into their confidence, weren't you?'

'Whose confidence?'

Sophie almost stamped her foot. 'Our parents' confidence, whose do you think?'

Simon cast an impatient look around them as though to reassure himself that their conversation was not being overheard. 'Where did you get all this?'

'From John.'

'John? What does he know about it?'

'Everything, apparently.'

'Then he should keep his mouth shut!'

'You understand what I'm talking about now, I take it.'

Simon heaved a sigh. 'It's all past history.'

'Is it?' Sophie drew her arm away from him. 'I don't agree.'

'It's not important.'

'Then why was I sent away?'

'In all probability you'd have gone to boarding school anyway——'

'Anyway,' she echoed bitterly.

'Well, I don't know why you're getting so steamed up about it.'

'I don't like the idea of my personal affairs being a matter for conjecture——'

'They weren't.' Simon stifled an expletive. 'And if that's what John Meredith told you, he's a liar!'

Sophie sighed. 'No——o, he didn't say that exactly,' she conceded. 'Oh, all right, let's forget it, shall we? Dance with me. The group has come back, and I feel like doing something completely outrageous!'

Simon pulled her towards him. 'Kiss me, then. That should dispel conjecture about you and Rob, once and for all.'

Sophie was tempted, but she pressed her palms against his chest, drawing back. 'No, Simon,' she said quietly, shaking her head. 'You're too nice to be made use of.'

Towards the end of the evening the Reverend Mr. Evans came up to them at the end of a particularly strenuous session of dancing. He smiled at Sophie and then turning to Simon, said: 'I've been meaning to ask you, Simon. Would you be prepared to show that collection of slides you took of Devon and Cornwall to my Women's Guild? Your headmaster told me you'd given a talk to your top junior classes, and he was very impressed. It's just the sort of thing we need, and it's so difficult to get interesting speakers. We've managed to rope in Mrs. Tarrant before she leaves for Greece, but come the autumn we've got nothing to offer.'

Simon glanced humorously at Sophie. 'Well,' he hesitated. 'I suppose I—could. But I'm not a professional speaker, you know.'

'Mrs. Tarrant?' Sophie was speaking now. 'Is that Harriet Tarrant, the historian?'

The vicar nodded. 'Why, yes. Do you know her, Sophie?'

'Oh, no.' Sophie shook her head. 'But I was reading an article about her in the paper last weekend. I was interested, that's all. I took Greek at Ordinary level and I find her books fascinating.'

'Would you like to meet her?' The vicar was clearly disarmed by her enthusiasm.

'Oh, I would,' Sophie nodded.

'Come with me, then. She's over here somewhere. When she's at home, she often attends my little gatherings.'

Sophie raised her eyebrows meaningfully at Simon and he followed her and the vicar across the hall to where several older people were sitting in a group, talking. Most of them Sophie knew by sight through her father's profession, but a plump, trouser-suited figure with a coil of mousy grey hair was unfamiliar.

'Harriet,' said Mr. Evans, attracting her attention, 'there's someone here who would like to meet you—Sophie Kemble. Doctor Kemble's daughter.'

The purple-clad figure rose to her feet and excusing herself from the others she joined the vicar and his two companions.

'How nice,' she enthused, when introductions were over, 'to find someone—some *young* person, that is—who understands Greek. Nowadays, youngsters seem to gravitate towards the simpler languages—French and German and Italian—and forget all about Latin and Greek, the classical languages.'

'I'm not much good at Latin, I'm afraid,' confessed Sophie, smiling.

'But you like Greek. And you're interested in mythology, eh?' Harriet glanced at the vicar and then back at Sophie again. 'You're not looking for a job, by any chance, are you?'

Sophie was taken aback, and it was Simon who answered for her. 'Sophie is going to university next year.'

'Are you? Are you really?' Harriet stared at her with piercing blue eyes. 'And what do you plan to do until then?'

Sophie lifted her shoulders helplessly. 'I—er—I haven't given the matter a lot of thought.'

'Then perhaps you should.' Harriet was nothing if not forthright. 'I'm prepared to offer you a job. I need a translator. Someone who knows more than *kalimera* and *parakalo*.'

Sophie looked questioningly at Simon and he said: 'I don't think my—that is, Sophie's father expects her to take a job, Mrs. Tarrant.'

'Why not? She needs the money, doesn't she?'

Sophie interposed: 'It's very kind of you to offer——'

'Nonsense, it's not kind at all.' Harriet Tarrant flexed her shoulder muscles. 'I need a translator, and it seems to me you'd be ideal for the job.'

Sophie licked her lips. 'And—what would it entail, Mrs. Tarrant?'

Harriet thrust her square hands into the pockets of her jacket, warming to her subject. 'It would entail spending half the year in Greece, for a start. I prefer to work there. I allow the atmosphere to absorb me. Then I have two researchers—Greeks, you understand —and they have been gathering material for me while I've been over here lecturing. When I go back there'll be a mound of material to read and evaluate, articles to translate, correspondence to deal with——'

'I don't type, Mrs. Tarrant.'

'Nonsense, anyone can type.' Harriet dismissed her protest with a shrug of her shoulders. 'I don't want a secretary, Sophie. A secretary with only commercial experience and an aptitude for typing would be of no use to me. No, what I need is someone who knows the legends, who can appreciate the precarious balance between fact and fantasy, and most of all, someone who can read and speak the language.'

It was a great temptation, Sophie couldn't deny that, even while she accepted that to put so many hundreds of miles between herself and Robert would tear her emotions to shreds. But sooner or later he would accept an overseas assignment and by then he and Emma would be married and his wife might go with him ... The prospect sent a prickling of goose-lumps over her skin. How would she stand the knowledge that they were living together, sleeping together ...

Noticing how pale Sophie had suddenly become, Simon said: 'I think perhaps we ought to be going, Sophie.'

The concern was eloquent in his tones and Harriet Tarrant's lips thinned. 'Well, Sophie?' she challenged. 'Do you want to think about it? I can give you a few days if you'd like to discuss the matter with your parents.'

Sophie hesitated. 'I—I would like to think about it,' she admitted, ignoring Simon's disapproval. 'Can I ring you? When I've come to a decision?'

'Of course.'

While Harriet wrote out her address and telephone number the vicar distracted Simon by confirming the promise he had gleaned from him earlier, saying how delighted the Women's Guild would be to have their first speaker for the new season already lined up.

But once they had put several feet between themselves and the others Simon turned on Sophie angrily. 'What do you mean by telling that woman you'd think over her proposition? You can't accept it, you know you can't!'

Sophie lifted her face up to his. 'Why not?'

Simon glared angrily about him. 'I don't want you to. Good lord, it was bad enough knowing Rob had——' He broke off and then went on: 'I don't want some oily Greek laying his hands on you!'

'Oh, Simon!'

'Don't "Oh, Simon" me! Besides, your father will never agree.'

'I shouldn't be too sure of that.' Sophie sounded almost cynical. 'Isn't this exactly the sort of opportunity which will appeal to him? Something to remove my disruptive influence from Robert's orbit?'

'*Robert!*'

Simon spoke his brother's name contemptuously, and suddenly Sophie felt incredibly weary. The noise of the electric guitars had become an increasing assault on her hearing, and a dull ache was spreading from her nape to the crown of her head.

'I think I would like to go home, Simon,' she said quietly, massaging her temples with her fingertips.

Simon looked as though he was about to protest and then with a sigh he nodded. Indicating that she should follow him, he began to force a way through the press of people near the door. John Meredith's crowd were there, but Sophie avoided visual confrontation. However, Emma had seen them, and she pushed her way towards them.

'Are you leaving?'

Simon said they were and Emma gave a sigh of relief.

'Oh, good. I'll come with you, then. I've had enough. The noise...' She shook her head expressively. 'Besides, it's not the same without Robbie.'

Sophie made some noncommittal reply and went to get her wrap from the cloakroom. No matter what Simon said, leaving Conwynneth was not such a bad idea.

CHAPTER SEVEN

IN the event, the decision whether or not to accept Harriet Tarrant's offer had to be postponed. The day following the dance at the village hall, Sophie awakened with a streaming cold, and by lunch time it was apparent that she should never have left her bed. Her father ordered her back there when he came in for his midday meal, and by late afternoon her temperature was well over a hundred. She spent the following week in bed, sick and feverish, and totally incapable of making any plans for her immediate future.

Naturally, although sympathetic towards her condition, Simon was delighted at the setback. Apparently uncaring that he might catch Sophie's germs, he spent hours in her room, reading and talking to her, and generally making her feel less isolated than she undoubtedly would have done. The only flaw in their relationship was John Meredith, who, having not been informed of her indisposition, called the evening after the dance to take Sophie to dinner. When he discovered that she was ill, he started enquiring about her every day, and sent masses of flowers to fill her room with their perfume. The Kembles approved of his attentions no more than did Simon, but short of being rude there was nothing they could do.

Emma was leaving at the weekend, and she came in on Sunday morning before she left to say goodbye. Simon was driving her back to London and she was already wearing her coat when she came to Sophie's room. Circumstances being what they were, this was the first time the two girls had been alone together, and in her weakened condition Sophie felt in no state to sustain a conversation.

However, Emma was clearly loath to risk contracting any kind of infection, and hovering near the door, said: 'I hope you'll be up and about again soon, Sophie. It's a shame being in bed when the weather's so lovely. Still, you have got some beautiful flowers, haven't you?'

Sophie plucked at the coverlet. 'I'm sure Daddy will allow me up next week.'

'I expect he will.' Emma fingered the door handle. 'And you do have your holiday to look forward to, don't you? Brittany. It should be rather nice. Robbie and I may come and join you all for a few days.'

She smiled, and Sophie concentrated hard on the eyelet stitching of the bedspread. It was such a smug smile, but perhaps she, Sophie, only saw it like that. She chided herself. Emma was a nice girl. It was she who distorted her image with her own frustrations.

Forcing herself to look up, she said: 'Have you enjoyed your holiday?'

Emma moved her shoulders in a dismissing motion. 'I suppose so. There's not much to do here, though, is there?'

Sophie looked towards her windows. 'I suppose it depends on what one enjoys doing.'

Emma's smile became a little fixed. 'Do I detect a note of censure?'

Sophie's head jerked round. 'No. No, of course not. I only meant—well, there's plenty to do if you enjoy walking and climbing—and playing golf and tennis.'

'Yes.' Emma sounded slightly bored. 'Well, I'm afraid I'm not the outdoor type.'

Sophie was tempted to ask what type she was, but decided against it. It would sound sarcastic, and the last thing she wanted was to enter into any kind of verbal fencing with Emma. She simply wasn't strong enough. So she said: 'I suppose living in London you tend to rely on artificial entertainments.'

It was an innocent enough remark, but Emma didn't choose to take it that way. 'What do you mean?' she enquired curtly.

Sophie sought for suitable words. 'Why, I only meant that living alone you must enjoy the excitement —the company that can be found in theatres, restaurants, that sort of thing.'

'But I don't live alone,' retorted Emma coldly. 'Oh, I realise you'd like to think so. But the fact is that when Robbie is there we don't need anyone else. Our own— company—is enough.'

Sophie swallowed hard, aware of a heightening of tension all over her body that brought her out in a cold sweat. What was Emma saying? Did it matter? She mustn't get involved...

'I didn't mean—that is——' she began, but Emma interrupted her, her smile quite disappeared now.

'Oh, yes, you did. Do you think I'm blind, Sophie? Do you think I'm stupid? Do you think I don't know how you feel about Robbie? I've seen the way you look at him, the way you speak to him——'

'Emma! Emma! Are you nearly ready?'

Simon's voice drifted up the stairs spelling blessed release for Sophie. Emma stepped on to the landing. 'Yes, I'm ready, Simon,' she called. 'I won't be a minute.' She turned back into the bedroom. 'Do hurry and get better, Sophie, won't you? I'm expecting you to be my chief bridesmaid, you know!' And with her usual cloying smile she was gone, her heels echoing down the stairs.

Simon couldn't understand why Emma's departure should have had such a singularly depressing effect on

Sophie. He had expected her to improve rapidly once the other girl was out of the house, but it was not so. Sophie was more morose than ever.

During the following week her naturally healthy body reasserted itself, however, and inevitably by the weekend she was physically well enough to get up and about again. A spell of warm weather made the garden an ideal place for convalescence, and Sophie spent hours lying listlessly on a lounger, listening to her transistor radio. Simon chivvied her for her lack of energy, but Doctor Kemble insisted that the rest would do her good.

The following Tuesday morning, John Meredith put in an appearance. Laura was loath to admit him, until he explained that he had a message for Sophie from Harriet Tarrant.

The proposal that Sophie might accept Harriet Tarrant's invitation to work for her for a year had been shelved for the period of Sophie's illness, and as Laura's only knowledge of it had come from Simon she was not enthusiastic that any decision should be made without first consulting her husband. Sophie herself had said nothing, but then she had hardly been in a condition to do so. Laura's initial reaction had been one of approval, but she had tempered this with the realisation that her husband might see it differently and therefore it would have to be approached with caution. She had intended discussing it with him for the past few evenings, but somehow the right moment had not presented itself. And now here was John Meredith with a message which might convey anything.

With a faint smile, she invited him into the lounge and went to find her stepdaughter.

Sophie was not yet dressed when Laura entered her bedroom. She was seated at the vanity unit in her cotton wrapper, brushing her hair. Her eyes widened at her stepmother's unexpected appearance, and she looked at her expectantly.

Laura closed the door. 'Oh, John's here,' she said, by way of an explanation.

Sophie rose to her feet. 'Is he?'

'Yes.' Laura rubbed her palms together. 'He has a message for you. From Harriet Tarrant.'

Sophie had deliberately not thought about Harriet Tarrant's offer for the past few days. It was too appealing in her weakened state, and she had no wish to do something on the spur of the moment which she would live to regret. But she also knew that Laura was waiting for some sort of explanation.

Taking off her wrapper to reveal her slenderness in a tan-coloured slip which matched her colouring, she reached for the lemon shirt and navy skirt she had laid out on the bed. 'I suppose you're wondering why Mrs. Tarrant should be sending a message to me.'

Laura shook her head. 'Not exactly. Simon told me you'd met her at the dance last week.'

'Oh, I see.' Sophie stepped into her skirt and zipped it up. 'I suppose he also told you that she'd offered me a job.'

'He did. But he wasn't enthusiastic. Are you?'

Sophie slipped her arms into the sleeves of her blouse. 'I'm not sure.'

'What do you mean?'

'I don't know.' Sophie shrugged, buttoning her blouse with automatic fingers. 'It's appealing—working in Greece, I mean. But I don't know whether I want to go away again. I've only just come home.'

Laura compressed her lips. 'It's a wonderful opportunity.'

For what?

For an awful moment Sophie thought she had said

118

the words aloud. But one look at her stepmother's face assured her that she hadn't.

'Yes,' she murmured, turning away to run the brush through her hair once more. 'Do I look all right?'

Laura hid her impatience. 'You look pale. But it suits you. Besides, you're not interested in impressing John Meredith, are you?'

Sophie waited for Laura to open the door. 'Where is he?'

'In the lounge. I'll get Mrs. Forrest to bring you some coffee. You've had no breakfast again.'

'I'm not hungry. But some coffee would be lovely.'

Sophie forced a smile, and leaving Laura behind ran down the stairs.

John rose to his feet as she entered the lounge, his eyes travelling intently over her. 'Pale, but interesting,' he commented lightly. 'Tell me, was it necessary to take to your bed to avoid a date with me?'

Sophie relaxed. She had forgotten how easy John was to talk to. 'I've been quite ill, actually,' she replied indignantly. 'And I'm sorry we missed our date.'

'Are you? Good. Then you won't object if I make another?'

Sophie swung herself down into an armchair, curling one leg gracefully beneath her. 'You have a message for me,' she reminded him.

'Yes,' John nodded. 'From our local historian, Mrs. Tarrant. She dined with us last evening and—er— your name came into the conversation.'

'She told you she'd offered me a job.' It was a statement.

'Mmm—mm. She seemed quite keen. Your knowledge of Greek appears to have endeared you to her. Are you going to take the job?'

Sophie looked down at her fingernails. 'I haven't decided yet. Is that what she sent you to ask me?'

'No. That was my question. But Corfu is such a long way away.'

'Corfu?'

'That's right. You know Mrs. Tarrant works in Corfu, don't you?'

'No. The actual location wasn't mentioned.' Sophie looked up. 'So what is the message?'

John seated himself opposite her. 'Nothing dramatic. Just to let you know that she's leaving for London this morning and she won't be back until the middle of next week. I think she was afraid you would try and get in touch with her while she was away and imagine she had already left for Greece.'

'Oh, I see.' Sophie was surprised at the relief she felt. Her decision could wait for a few more days at least.

Mrs. Forrest appeared with their coffee and while she set it down on a low table near Sophie, John asked her how her husband and family were keeping. Sophie thought he was very much the squire's son at that moment. But he was very likeable.

'So—down to more interesting matters,' he remarked, after the daily had left them and Sophie was pouring the coffee. 'Have dinner with me tomorrow evening.'

Sophie gasped. 'You don't waste much time, do you?'

'Time's money, as my dear father would say.'

'Even so . . .' Sophie chuckled. 'Anyway, that reminds me, I haven't thanked you for all the flowers you sent while I was ill. They were gorgeous.'

'I'm glad you liked them.' John grinned at her as he accepted his coffee. 'I suppose that's my cue to say that none of them could be as gorgeous as you.'

Sophie shook her head laughingly. She felt better at that moment than she had done for days. And when the door opened behind them, she felt no premonition of apprehension glancing round. She had expected to meet her stepmother's disapproving stare, but instead she encountered Robert's cold and angry face.

Almost at the same moment, John became aware of the advent of the newcomer, and he rose awkwardly to his feet, conscious that in some way he was responsible for Robert's grim countenance.

'Hey, Rob,' he greeted the other man warmly. 'What are you doing here?'

Robert came into the room, his movements lithe and controlled, like the movements of a panther. 'This is my home, John,' he informed him coldly. 'Why shouldn't I be here?'

John spread his hands apologetically and Sophie could feel the tension building. 'I wasn't questioning your right to be here, man. I'm surprised to see you, that's all.'

Robert inhaled deeply, looking down at the tray of coffee, and Sophie allowed herself to look at him. In cream suede pants and a cream silk shirt he was disturbingly attractive. The tight trousers clung to his thighs, emphasising the strong muscles there, drawing her attention to the long powerful legs. Her eyes drifted up over lean hips, a broadening expanse of chest beneath the clinging shirt, a strong throat, deeply tanned like his face. His face ... her eyes encountered his and she flinched away from the cold, calculating fury she glimpsed there.

'How are you, Sophie?' he enquired politely, and she was astonished at the calmness of his tone. It disconcerted her, and her reply was jerky and stammered:

'I—er—I'm—much—much better, thank you.'

Robert returned his attention to John, much to Sophie's relief. 'At the risk of repeating your words— what are you doing here?'

'I came to see Sophie.' John shrugged his shoulders.

'To see if she was better, and to bring her a message.'

'A message?' Robert raised his eyebrows sardonically. 'I wouldn't have seen you in the role of a messenger boy, John.'

It was his tone rather than his words which was offensive and John's expression hardened. 'Perhaps not. But then I wouldn't have seen you in the guise of the heavy father either.'

Sophie rose abruptly to her feet. She was sick and tired of Robert picking arguments with other people in her company. 'John doesn't have to report his behaviour to you, Robert,' she declared, her hands clenched into fists by her sides. 'You have no right to come in here and behave as if we were committing some kind of crime! I have been ill, and John has been enquiring after my health! What are you doing home, anyway? I should have thought that as Emma has left you'd have spent your free time in London— with your fiancée!'

It cost her a lot to say that, but it had the desired effect. With a contemptuous look at both of them, Robert turned and strode out of the room, slamming the door behind him.

'Phew!' John made a pretence of wiping his brow. 'That was a close shave!'

Sophie tried to smile. 'Don't be silly.'

John shook his head. 'I'm not. That stepbrother of yours would make mincemeat of me. I know—I saw him in action while we were at university.'

Sophie paced restlessly to the windows, looking out on the lawns at the front of the house. 'I'm sorry. I don't know what's wrong with him.'

'I do.' John thrust his hands into his pockets. 'He's jealous!'

'Jealous?' Sophie turned to stare at him incredulously. 'You're not serious!'

'I am.' John came to stand beside her. 'It's not un-usual, Sophie. For years you've been Robert's devoted slave, his fervent admirer—hanging on his every word. Sooner or later you were bound to grow up, to make new friends, friends of the opposite sex.'

'Oh, John!'

'Well? Naturally, Rob doesn't like it. It's usurping his authority. Like the rest of us, he's selfish with the things he cares about.'

'But I'm not a *thing*! I'm a person.'

'Exactly. And Rob's just beginning to appreciate that. The fact that he's engaged is tying his hands more securely.'

Sophie digested this silently. It was possible that there was some truth in what John was saying, but it did not help her. For a moment—for a heart-stopping moment—when John had said that Robert was jeal-ous, she had foolishly imagined he meant something entirely different, something infinitely more personal. But of course, John was right. If Robert was jealous of her friendship with John and Simon, it was a purely selfish reaction. He didn't want her himself, but he didn't care for anyone else to have her either.

'I think I'd better be going away,' said John, at last. 'I don't want to run into Simon on my way out.'

Sophie's lips twitched. 'Stop teasing.'

'All right. Now about tomorrow evening?'

'Do you still want to take me out?'

John grinned. 'Forewarned is forearmed, as they say. I'll be wearing my pigskin knuckledusters and packing a water pistol.'

Sophie giggled. 'Oh, John! You're good for me, do you know that?'

John caught her chin with one hand and studied her face intently. 'You could be good for me, too, Sophie,' he murmured huskily, and then dropped his hand and turned away. 'Tomorrow night. Seven-thirty.'

'All right,' Sophie nodded, and he left her saying he could let himself out.

After he had gone, Sophie put their dirty coffee cups back on the tray and picking it up carried it through to the kitchen. Laura was there, but so, too, was Mrs. Forrest, and her stepmother accompanied her back into the lounge. 'Well?' she urged. 'What was the message?'

Sophie made a casual gesture. 'Nothing important. Mrs. Tarrant has gone away for a few days. She didn't want me to try and contact her unsuccessfully.'

'Was that all?' Laura looked disappointed. 'Couldn't she have telephoned?'

'I expect she could. But as she was dining with the Merediths last night, I suppose John offered to let me know himself.' She paused. 'By the way, I'm having dinner with him tomorrow evening.'

Laura was taken aback. 'I see. I thought your father and I made our opinion of your association with John Meredith clear enough while you were ill.'

'I like him,' said Sophie steadily.

'He's much too old for you. And besides, he's engaged.'

'That's his affair, surely.'

'Sophie!' Laura tapped her palms irritably together. 'What is the matter with you? Ever since you arrived home you seem to have taken a delight in disrupting this household!'

'I'm sorry.'

Laura sighed impatiently. 'Oh, my dear, I don't want to quarrel with you, but——' She halted. 'Do you know Robert's home?'

Sophie stiffened. 'Yes.'

'I suppose he came and had a few words with John.'

'You could say that.'

Laura frowned. 'Why do you sound so sarcastic?'

'No reason.' Sophie sagged. 'I'm tired, Mummy. Do you mind if I go and sit in the garden for a while?'

Laura clicked her tongue. 'Oh, I suppose not.' She shook her head in apparent confusion. 'I don't know what things are coming to.'

Mrs. Forrest had already unfolded the lounger and left it in Sophie's favourite position beneath the wide branches of the oak. She stretched her legs wearily and felt a sense of impatience at her own weakness. Lying in bed had taken its toll of her strength, but the mental energy consumed in her confrontation with Robert had been the telling factor.

She wondered how long she would take to feel completely recovered. Perhaps by the time Mrs. Tarrant returned from London she would feel strong enough to make the decision about her future. Right now, it had never seemed more nebulous.

The sun glinted down through the branches of the tree and she closed her eyes. She could hear the steady humming of the bees among her stepmother's sweet peas, and the occasional squabbling of the birds in the branches overhead. From the house she could hear the sound of Mrs. Forrest vacuuming the bedrooms. The windows were all wide and she could vaguely distinguish the sound of voices in the study.

She had been lying there perhaps half an hour when she realised that the voices droning on the stillness of the air were gradually getting louder. She couldn't hear what was being said, but she could recognise the antagonists now as her stepmother and Robert.

Her nerves tightened and a wave of apprehension swept over her body. Her eyes opened and she looked down with dislike at her fingers gripping the arms of the chair. Calm down, she told herself fiercely. It's probably nothing to do with you.

But what were they arguing about? It was obvious from the tone of their voices that anger was simmering near the surface. She felt her whole body tense as a sudden silence ensued, but then the voices broke out as before, louder now, still not close enough for her to hear the words but sharper.

She realised as feet crunched on gravel that they were at the front of the house. There was an altercation and then the heavy slamming of a car door. Sophie sat upright, her mouth suddenly dry as the powerful engine roared to life. Whatever else was exchanged was lost in the shattering squeal of protesting tyres, as the Jensen took off down the drive. Sophie found she was trembling and endeavoured to get control of herself. So what? Robert was gone again. But where? And for how long?

CHAPTER EIGHT

ALTHOUGH her stepmother looked rather distraught at lunch time, no mention was made of the row she had had with Robert and Sophie was surprised. Instead, Laura made light of his visit, telling her husband and Simon that he had merely called in on his way to London. Simon had spent the morning in Hereford, and Sophie couldn't help feeling relieved that he had not been involved.

Of Sophie's intention to go out with John Meredith, Laura was much more coherent, and Doctor Kemble added his disapproval to that of his wife and stepson. 'I don't blame you entirely, Sophie,' he said heavily. 'Meredith should have more sense than to go around making assignations with other girls of good family.'

Sophie pushed her half-eaten steak aside. 'Does that mean that if I was not of good family it wouldn't matter?'

'Don't speak to your father in that way!' Laura's lips were drawn in.

Sophie coloured and her father sighed. 'I can manage this, thank you, Laura,' he stated, considering the wine in his glass. 'Sophie, why do you want to go out with this man? Good heavens, aren't there enough young men of your own age around?'

'Young men of my own age bore me!' retorted Sophie mutinously.

Doctor Kemble shook his head. 'It's only to be expected, I suppose. You've been too much in the company of Robert and Simon——'

'That's not true!' exclaimed Sophie indignantly.

'I've been at boarding school almost five years. I mixed with plenty of boys there.' She looked down at her hands folded in her lap. 'And in any case, I like John. He's——' she glanced awkwardly at Simon, 'he's good company.'

Mrs. Forrest's appearance with the dessert successfully diverted the conversation and only Simon took it up later when he and Sophie were lounging in the garden together.

'You know,' he said confidentially, 'Rob wouldn't like the idea of you getting involved with John Meredith, any more than the rest of us.'

Sophie expelled her breath resentfully. 'Do you think I care what Robert likes?'

Simon tugged absently at a blade of grass. 'Yes, I think you do.'

Sophie turned her shoulder to him and stared moodily across the lawn. 'I think I will accept Mrs. Tarrant's offer of a job,' she said bitterly. 'Then I'll be out of everyone's hair.'

'Oh, stop talking rubbish!' Simon's fingers dug into her shoulder as he swung her round to face him. 'You know perfectly well that Rob's at the bottom of everything—your attitude to John, your resentment against the parents, the temptation to take Mrs. Tarrant's offer and escape. Do you think that will solve anything? Running away, I mean?'

Sophie's mouth trembled. 'What do you suggest I do, then? Live here as a recluse?'

'Of course not.' Simon released her. 'I suggest you start thinking about your future—your real future, not the immediate few months.'

'A job with Mrs. Tarrant might last longer than a few months.'

'What do you mean? That you'd throw up your studies to become a—a translator? Somebody else's assistant, when you've got the ability to get a degree yourself?'

'It would be interesting work, Simon. I'd enjoy it.'

'Enjoy it!' he growled angrily. 'What a waste!'

'Well, what about you?' she countered. 'You're not ambitious. You're quite content to work in Conwynneth.'

'That's different.'

'How is it different?'

'I'm not like you—or Rob. I've got no brilliant brain working for me. I know my limitations.'

'And perhaps I know mine.'

'You could do it. I know you could.'

'In practical terms, yes. But what if I don't want to?'

Simon shredded the blade of grass he had torn up. 'Do you know what you do want?'

'I did.' Sophie's voice was low.

Simon looked sharply at her. 'Rob, I suppose.' When Sophie didn't answer, he kicked viciously at a clump of daisies. 'Well, Rob's going to marry Emma, and the sooner you accept that, the better.'

Sophie hunched her shoulders. 'Do you think I haven't?'

Simon uttered an imprecation. 'You should have known it was no good. The parents were always against it.'

'I didn't know that until just recently, you may remember,' she reminded him tremulously. Then the need to hurt him as he had just hurt her overcame scruples. 'If that's so, why do you say you want me? Surely the same criterion will apply.'

Simon's lips twisted. 'Ah, but I'm prepared to use a little strategy. I'm in no hurry. I can wait. I can wait until you've taken your degree, made something of your life. A lot can happen in five or six years, and a woman in her twenties is a different proposition from a teenage girl.'

Sophie turned away from him again. His cool, calculated planning was distasteful to her. Did his mother know how he felt? Would she be in agreement when the time came?

'I—I might meet someone at university,' she said, not looking at him. 'University or Greece—I don't see the difference so far as you're concerned.'

'At university you'd still be in England—accessible, in other words. And if you found someone else——' He shrugged. 'I'd face that when I came to it.'

'Oh, Simon, don't talk like this.' She put her fingers over her ears. 'You can't arrange people's lives for them.'

Simon rose to his feet. 'I promised the vicar I'd take those slides over to show him this afternoon. Do you want to come?'

Sophie shook her head, not looking up, and with a grimace Simon walked away. Sophie watched surreptitiously until he had disappeared into the house and then lay back on the lounger. Was she never to cease being shocked by her family's duplicity? Robert, Laura, Simon—they all tried to manipulate people to their own ends.

The following evening John took Sophie to dine at an hotel on the outskirts of Hereford. It was quite a large place, newly opened and popular, and several people recognised and spoke to them as they took their seats in the restaurant. Knowing herself to be the cynosure of several pairs of eyes made Sophie nervous, but John soon put her at her ease with his amusing banter. His eyes told her she was attractive, and his good humour showed that he was enjoying himself. And indeed, Sophie had taken pains with her appearance in defiance of the family's disapproval. Her dress was the second of the gowns Laura had bought for her while Emma was staying with them, and although at the time they had acquired it Sophie had thought it the least attractive of the two, she had now revised her opinion. It was very plain, and made of white crêpe jersey, but only this evening had she realised how it moulded the swelling curves of her slender figure and threw the honey gold of her tan into relief. If nothing else, it assured her that she was a woman, and not the child she was sometimes regarded as.

After the meal they sat in the attractive bar lounge with its barrel-shaped bar and swinging coloured lights. They talked about inconsequential things mostly—films and television, books they had read, places they had visited. It was all very easy and relaxing and Sophie really enjoyed herself.

They drove back to Conwynneth soon after ten and by mutual consent parked the car at the end of the drive so that John escorted her the final few yards on foot. The house looked dark and deserted and she recalled that her parents and Simon had planned to go to the Pages that evening. It was still quite early. Obviously they weren't home yet.

In the porch of the house, Sophie turned to John gratefully, her silvery hair swinging softly about her shoulders. 'I've had a wonderful evening,' she said warmly, touching his arm. 'Thank you for being so nice.'

Even in the gloom, Sophie saw his mouth twitching with amusement. 'I'm sure that's an adjective calculated to choke off the most ardent suitor!' he mocked. 'Nice! Oh, yes, I must remember that.'

Sophie giggled. 'You know what I mean. You are nice. I only wish——' She broke off, and opening her bag rummaged around for the key she always kept there. She brought it out triumphantly, and then looked up at him again. 'Well, goodnight, John.'

John frowned. 'Is no one at home?'

'I don't think so. My parents are spending the evening at the Pages'. They'll be home soon.'

'Do you want me to come in with you?'

Sophie hesitated. 'I—no, I don't think so, thank you. They wouldn't—like it.'

John nodded. 'Okay, so we say goodnight here. Goodnight, Sophie.' And before she could stop him, he bent his head and implanted a firm kiss on her mouth.

She gasped when he let her go, because almost at the same moment a light was switched on in the hall of the house, illuminating the porch with unexpected brilliance. She looked at John again and made a helpless little gesture. 'Obviously I was wrong. They are home.'

John looked doubtful. 'Are you sure? You don't want me to check and find out?'

'Why? You don't think—oh, *no*!' Sophie's face revealed her disbelief. 'No thief would turn on all the lights.' Then she gathered herself. 'Well, there's one way to find out.' She turned the handle of the door and it opened inwards. 'You see—it's not locked.' She stepped into the hall. 'Daddy! Mummy, I'm home!'

Her father's study door was open and she walked rather gingerly towards it, ridiculing herself for the faint sense of apprehension she was feeling. 'Daddy...' She said again, tentatively. 'Is that you?'

She almost took a step backward when a man did emerge from the study, but it wasn't her father. It was Robert. 'Hello, Sophie,' he said bleakly, his gaze moving beyond her to John still standing on the porch, one foot raised to rest on the step as though poised to jump to Sophie's aid should that be necessary. 'Hello, John. I thought it might be you.'

John looked taken aback. 'I understood from the

vicar that you left yesterday morning, Rob. What are you making? A series of flying visits, or is Emma with you?'

The introduction of Emma's name was deliberate and Sophie tensed. But all Robert did was shake his head. 'I'm alone, John. Literally alone.' His eyes flickered to Sophie, moving over her without apparent pleasure. 'Where are the parents?'

'They're—they're at the Pages'.' Sophie's shoulders moved involuntarily. 'Simon, too, I think.'

'I see.' Robert looked again at John. 'Are you coming in or leaving right away?'

John raised his eyebrows. 'Do I have a choice?'

Robert made a negative gesture. 'That's up to Sophie, I suppose.' And he turned and went back into the study, closing the door with a definite click.

John shook his head as though unable to understand his erstwhile friend's behaviour. 'Well, Sophie?'

'I think you'd better go,' said Sophie firmly, moving to the door and sliding her fingers over the handle. 'Thank you again for a lovely evening. I did enjoy it.'

'Good,' John nodded, pushing his hands into his trouser pockets. 'So did I.' He hesitated, looking as though he would like to say more. But then he turned away. 'Okay, Sophie, I'll be seeing you.'

Sophie closed the door behind him with some relief. It wasn't relief at his departure so much as relief that Robert had not chosen to cause any more trouble. She had the feeling that if she had invited John in, Robert would have appeared again, and the outcome did not bear thinking about.

With a little sigh, she dropped her evening bag on the hall table, kicked off her shoes and walked into the kitchen. She was thirsty and she knew there were some tins of ice-cold Coke in the refrigerator. She was pouring Coke into a glass when she became aware that she was being watched.

Robert was leaning against the door jamb, lean and arresting in a dark blue silk shirt and navy corded pants. He, too, was barefoot, evidence that he had been home for some time.

'He's gone,' he stated unnecessarily, glancing round the kitchen.

'Yes.' Sophie finished pouring the Coke and indicated the glass. 'Do you want some?'

Robert shook his head. 'Where have you been?'

Sophie forced herself to swallow some of the Coke before replying. She wasn't going to let him intimidate her, she *wasn't*. 'We had dinner at—at some hotel near Hereford. The Swan—is that right? Have you ever been there?'

'I suppose he invited you out while he was here yesterday.' Robert's tones were even, but there was an underlying note of menace which Sophie was not unaware of.

'I—yes, as a matter of fact, he did.' She paused. 'Actually, he invited me out a couple of weeks ago, but I was taken ill and—and couldn't make it.'

'Oh? When was that?'

Sophie took another determined sip of the Coke. 'We—that is, Simon and I went to a dance at the village hall. John and—and his fiancée were there. It—it was while Emma was here. They invited her to go with them. Did—didn't she tell you?'

Robert seemed disinclined to answer her questions. 'And do you like him?'

Sophie could feel herself colouring. 'What a question!' she managed lightly. 'Of course I like him.'

She was unprepared for Robert covering the space between them in two easy strides and dragging her round to face him, his hands cruelly hard as they gripped her forearms. 'How much do you like him?' he demanded harshly. 'Tell me! I want to know.'

Sophie caught her breath, holding on to her glass with both hands, like a lifeline. Fortunately it was almost empty or she would have spilt the contents down her dress.

'I—I just—like him,' she got out unsteadily.

'As you like Simon?' He paused. 'Or me?'

Sophie struggled to free herself. 'I don't think it's any of your business.'

'Don't you?' He wrenched the glass out of her fingers and thrust it impatiently aside. Then he hauled her closer to him, so close that she could feel the stirring warmth of his masculinity through the soft material of her gown. 'Sophie, I'm not asking out of idle curiosity,' he muttered hoarsely. 'I don't have some perverted streak that demands you reveal your innermost feelings to me. But——' He hesitated, looking down the neckline of her dress to where the hollow between her breasts cast a tantalising shadow. 'I have to know, Sophie. I have to know whether in the company of John—or Simon—or someone like them, you can forget the things we said to one another on the river bank a few weeks ago!'

Sophie gazed up at him, and his eyes lifted to encounter hers. Her eyes were wide and troubled, and her fingers sought futilely to lever his from her arms. 'How—how can you ask me that?' she choked. 'Oh, how can you?'

Robert continued to stare down at her as though he would penetrate her very soul, and then with a groan, he nodded. 'That's all I wanted to know.'

He released her arms and would have slid his arms around her then, but she took the moment of weakness to break free of him, backing away to the wall behind her. 'Please,' she begged, her breath coming low and shallowly. 'Go away and leave me alone.' She turned her head desperately from side to side. 'I don't know what you want of me, but I can't give it.'

Robert came towards her, ignoring the appeal in her voice, the tremor that revealed her state of emotion. He backed her up against the wall and then placed one hand on either side of her, successfully blocking any escape. His dark face was sombre, and although she could not be unaware of his physical sensuality his thoughts were successfully veiled by the thickness of his lashes.

Having trapped his prey, Robert seemed in no hurry to go further, in a physical sense, that is. On the contrary, he seemed to gain a certain amount of satisfaction from just watching the play of emotions over her expressive face, the rise and fall of her breasts beneath the thin material of her gown, exulting in his power over her. Sophie's palms were pressed against the wall at her sides and the tension of the past few weeks was tightening like a physical knot in her stomach.

'Oh, *please*,' she entreated him urgently. 'Robert, let me go!'

For an answer he lowered his body against hers, his lean thighs demanding an intimacy which she had no strength—or will—to deny him. Then he bent his head, his mouth seeking and finding hers. His fingers parted her lips, cupping her face, probing the curve of her nose and cheeks, the hidden hollows of her ears. He reached for her hands, drawing them up to his body as though she had the right to do with him as she willed. With a little sob, she wound herself against him, responding with an abandonment that would shock her when she thought about it later, not much caring that their parents might come home at any time and find them like this.

And, in fact, it was the sound of her father's car in

the drive that brought Sophie to her senses. Weakened as he was by the demands of his own body, Robert was in no state to stop her when she dragged herself away from him and escaped to the lounge before the front door opened. She had the sense to close the kitchen door behind her as she went, giving Robert a little more time to pull himself together. When her step-mother came to the door of the lounge, she found Sophie curled up in an armchair apparently intent on reading a copy of *Country Life*.

'We saw the lights,' remarked Laura, coming in and taking off the shawl she had been wearing about her shoulders. 'We knew you must be home.'

Sophie cleared her throat. 'As—as a matter of fact, Robert was home—before me,' she said.

A frown drew Laura's brows together. 'Robert? He's here?' And at Sophie's nod: 'Where is he?'

Doctor Kemble and Simon were following her into the lounge now and Sophie took a moment to speak to them before replying in what she hoped was a casual tone: 'I—er—I think he's in the kitchen. I'm not sure.'

Laura looked at her husband. 'Robert's here,' she said blankly, going past him to find her elder son.

'Robert?' Doctor Kemble turned to Sophie. 'Robert's here?'

'Oh, yes!'

Sophie sounded irritable, but she couldn't help it. A rising surge of emotionalism was threatening to over-whelm her, and she took refuge in irritation. Now that she was recovering from that devastating interlude in the kitchen, a feeling of shame and self-disgust was sweeping over her. How could she have behaved so wantonly? she asked herself bitterly. How could she have let him touch her in such an intimate way? It was like Simon had said. Robert was a swine, making love to her while his fiancée was alone in London. Was he naturally promiscuous? She would not have thought so. Or was it simply that the thing that sprang between them was too strong for him to resist? The bond had always been there, she had to admit that. But she was a fool to allow him privileges which he obviously regarded in no serious way. If their parents had not arrived home as they did, might she have found the temptation to know his possession greater than she could resist? And if she had, what then...?

'How long have you been home, Sophie?' asked Simon, and she knew he was wondering how long she and Robert had been alone together.

She managed to shrug. 'I don't know exactly. Twenty minutes—half an hour, maybe. Why?'

'I just wondered.' Simon turned away, digging his hands into his jacket pockets. 'Does anyone want any coffee?'

Doctor Kemble was seating himself comfortably in his chair by the presently empty fire grate. He reached for his pipe and then looked up. 'What? Coffee? Hmm—yes, I could drink some. How about you, Sophie?'

Sophie uncurled herself. 'Not for me, thanks.' She rose to her feet. 'Would you mind if I went to bed, Daddy? I am rather—tired.'

'Not at all, my dear.' But Doctor Kemble's smile was rather anxious.

Sophie bent to kiss his cheek. 'See you in the morning. Goodnight, Simon.'

She heard the sound of Robert's and her stepmother's voices as she approached the kitchen, but she had to say goodnight as though nothing was wrong. Pushing open the door, she said: 'I'm going to bed, Mummy. Goodnight.'

Robert was standing by the fridge, drinking from a can of beer, but he lowered the can and wiped his mouth when he saw Sophie. Although she knew only

she was aware of it, there was still a vaguely lan-
guorous look in his eyes, a sensuous twist to his mouth.
Just looking at him she could feel rivers of emotion
running through her veins, moistening her palms,
weakening her knees. She wanted to go back into his
arms and stay there, and the knowledge brought the
hot flush of colour up her cheeks.

Fortunately, Laura was filling the kettle at the sink
and was too wrapped up with what she had been saying to Robert to pay a lot of attention to Sophie. She
scarcely glanced at the girl, saying shortly: 'All right,
Sophie. Goodnight!' without even offering her cheek
to be kissed as she usually did. Sophie closed the door
behind her and ran up the stairs to her room feeling
sick with reaction.

All the while she undressed and went into the bathroom to have a wash, she went over what had happened a dozen times. At school, in the seclusion of the
dorm at night, she had indulged herself in fantasies
about Robert, but never in her imagination had she
experienced the overwhelming surge of feeling he had
inspired in her tonight. It wasn't fair, she told herself
over and over again. It wasn't fair that he should
arouse her as he had and then expect her to behave as
though nothing had happened. No amount of shame
or self-recrimination could rid her of the memory of
the hungry possession of his mouth, or compensate for
the undoubted ecstasy complete surrender would bring.

She scrubbed hard at her teeth. One thing was becoming apparent—she would have to go away from
here, away from Robert's presence, away from the
devastating possibility that one day she might give in
to him, might lose all self-respect and any chance of
happiness with someone else. And if he should already
be married...

She clenched her lids tightly, feeling the hot wetness

of tears trickling down her cheeks. She must control herself, she thought fiercely. Crying would solve nothing. She must keep telling herself what kind of a man Robert really was.

She emerged from the bathroom with her head down, holding the folds of her wrapper closely about her. But instinct lifted her head and she halted at the sight of Robert leaning indolently against her open bedroom door. He straightened at her approach and said: 'I want to talk to you, Sophie.'

Sophie glanced automatically behind her. 'Does your mother know where you are?'

Robert's lips tightened. 'Come inside,' he said, standing back to allow her entrance. 'I don't intend to indulge in verbal skirmishing on the landing.'

Sophie still hesitated. 'I don't think you should be here at all,' she responded steadily. 'It's late. And I'm tired——'

'Damn you, come in here!' he muttered, losing patience and grasping her wrist, dragging her into the room. He released her to close the door, and she put the width of the bed between them.

'What do you want?'

Robert breathed heavily. 'That rather depends on you.'

'What do you mean?'

Robert looked down at his bare feet. 'I broke my engagement to Emma yesterday evening.'

'What?' Sophie couldn't believe her ears.

'You heard me.' He sighed. 'And you know why.'

Sophie's fingers were trembling so much she could hardly retain her hold on the sprigged wrapper. 'I'm not sure that I do.'

Robert raised his eyes heavenward for a moment. Then he looked at her again and her breathing quickened at the naked passion in his gaze. 'I love you,

Sophie,' he said, without emotion. 'I always have, and I guess I always will.'

Sophie plucked at the cord of her gown, jerking its narrow band about her waist. 'This—this is rather sudden, isn't it?' she asked, with a futile attempt at levity.

'Oh, stop it, Sophie!' Robert's nerves were clearly as stretched as hers. His fists clenched by his sides, and his face was pale beneath his tan. 'All right.' He took a deep breath. 'All right. You deserve an explanation, and I'll give you one.' He paused significantly. 'Your father and my mother are against our association. They always have been. They think I'm too old for you, and I am. No——' as she would have protested, '—let me finish. I thought so, too.'

'Robert——'

'Please, Sophie, let me go on.' He allowed his fists to uncurl. 'There were other factors, relevant factors, factors which could not be ignored. Your age was only one of them. We knew one another too well—or so they said. We'd been too close, you hadn't had the opportunity to meet other boys, have other relationships. They—the parents—insisted that I was not to get involved with you. And I accepted it. Two years ago, as I told you that day you arrived home from school, I despised myself for touching you. You were so young, you had your whole life in front of you. You still do...' His lips twisted. 'Well, anyway, I told the parents what had happened. I needed to salve my conscience, and in part I succeeded. While you were away, I could convince myself that everything they said was right. I told myself that in time I'd get over what I felt for you. I had to tell myself that, or I'd have gone mad!'

'Oh, Robert!' She would have gone to him then, but his hand gestured her to stay where she was.

'So my job was—is—interesting. You were at school.

141

I never allowed myself to dwell on the fact of its being a mixed establishment. I was away working during your holidays, and—and Emma was available.' He flexed his shoulder muscles wearily. 'I admit, I used Emma. But only because she wanted to be used.'

Sophie licked her dry lips. 'Did—did you ever tell Emma about—about me?'

Robert sighed again. 'Some. Once, in a weak, maudlin moment of sentimentality I confessed that I had—kissed you. I made light of it afterwards, but I think she guessed the rest.'

'And—and now?'

Robert shook his head. 'I can't go on with the engagement any longer. I'm not proud of my behaviour. When I got this job in Wales, I panicked.' He uttered a short mirthless laugh. 'I really panicked, do you know that? I knew you were due home for the holidays —that you might be home for some considerable time, and I couldn't trust myself!' His expression mirrored the self-derision he had felt. 'Well, I got drunk, good and drunk, and somehow during the course of that evening I asked Emma to marry me. I don't remember a lot about it, but I'm prepared to accept that I was desperate enough to do anything.' He raked a hand through his hair. 'That's about it, except that—I *was* supposed to tell you about the engagement when I came to meet you. And I would have, too, if that storm hadn't erupted. As it was...'

Sophie felt weak with suppressed emotion. 'And how —how did you feel afterwards?'

Robert uttered an expletive. 'How do you think I felt?' He scuffed his bare toes against the carpet. 'I tried to keep out of your way. I had been given some free time just when I could do without it.'

'You went up to London and saw Emma.'

'Yes, I did that a couple of times. She was working,

of course. I also went sailing with John—I did some survey work for the company—I went climbing. I tried to wear myself out so that when I went to bed I slept the sleep of the exhausted.' He hunched his shoulders. 'But it didn't work out.'

'So?'

'You were seeing a lot of Simon. I was as jealous as hell. Then when you went swimming at the Merediths'—— My God, I could have murdered John that day!'

Sophie gave a nervous smile. 'I think he knew it.'

'I'm sure he did.' Robert's face was sombre. 'So—I went against the parents' wishes and took you out myself. That day at Gloucester, I knew I couldn't go on pretending I didn't care. Then when we got home ...' He shuddered. 'I didn't know Emma was expected, I swear I didn't. My mother had invited her without my knowledge.' He bent his head. 'When I came to your room——' He broke off harshly. 'Well, anyway, as you may or may not know, there was one hell of a row that night.'

'I didn't know.'

'No. You only caught the aftermath, didn't you?'

'You left the following morning.'

'That's right.'

Sophie moved restlessly. 'I didn't know why. Your mother said you had gone to London, but that Emma was staying.'

'Yes—well, I spent the weekend at the flat, going over what had been said. The same arguments applied, but they no longer seemed relevant. Even so, your father has an innate ability to make the absurd sound reasonable. I was prepared to make an effort to see things his way.' He smoothed his palms down over his thighs. 'Then you were taken ill. Oh, none of the family informed me. I rang up to speak to my mother and Mrs. Forrest answered the phone. She told me. It was news, and Mrs. Forrest likes a gossip. Anyway, I got the truth out of my mother, and we had words on the subject. Even then, I stayed away. But eventually, when I did come to see you, what did I find? You taking coffee with John—enjoying his company instead of mine!'

'He said you were jealous.'

'And so I was. I was furious.' He shook his head reminiscently. 'That was when I knew this farce couldn't go on. I went and saw my mother—I told her I was going to break with Emma.'

'I think I heard you arguing.'

'No doubt you did. It was quite a blow to her to realise I was no longer prepared to consider her wishes before my own. I left for town right away. I saw Emma last night.'

Sophie tried to absorb what he was telling her. But it was very difficult. Was it possible that after all her heart-searching of the past few weeks everything was going to be as she had dreamed? Certainly it seemed so, and yet she would not have expected Emma to relinquish her claim quite so easily. She would have liked to have asked what Emma had said when he had told her he wanted to break the engagement. But of course, she could not. That was between Robert and his ex-fiancée and no one else.

Now Robert was straightening his shoulders, looking across at her steadily, silently demanding some kind of reaction. Sophie raised both hands, pressing the palms together in a gesture of supplication.

'And now?' she managed tremulously.

'Now...' Robert's mouth quirked. 'As I said, that's up to you. I've told my mother I've broken the engagement, and no doubt at this moment she's regaling your father with the news. So far as I'm concerned, what happens next is entirely up to you.'

Sophie took a tentative step towards him. Then she halted again. 'Did—did your mother tell you that I've been offered a job?'

Robert expelled his breath resignedly. 'Yes, she told me that. She told me while you were ill, as a matter of fact. She made it sound as though once you were better you would be taking it up.'

'Did she?' Sophie's stomach muscles knotted. Of course, she had suspected Laura might approve. It would certainly solve the problem of Sophie getting involved with her sons.

'How about you?' Robert's voice was cooler now. 'Does working in Greece appeal to you?'

Sophie's lips trembled. She could have laughed were it not so serious. *Did working in Greece appeal to her?* Compared with what? Compared with staying here and watching him marry Emma—yes. Compared with marrying Robert herself—oh, God, *no*! But he hadn't asked her to marry him yet, had he?

Lightly, so he should not suspect her extreme nervousness, she said: 'Do you have an alternative to offer?'

Robert's jaw clenched. 'Don't play games with me, Sophie!'

Her eyes widened. 'I'm not playing games. I—I just don't know what it is you want of me.'

'You don't *know*?' Robert reached her in seconds, pushing her down on the bed, and flinging himself beside her. 'What the hell do you think I've been telling you for the past few minutes?' he demanded savagely, winding her hair around his fingers, jerking her head cruelly. His mouth seared across the smooth curve of her throat, his teeth caught and held the lobe of her left ear. He moved so that one of his legs was imprisoning both of hers. 'You know what I want,

Sophie,' he groaned against her ear. 'I want you!' And his mouth crushed hers so that it opened beneath his like a yielding blossom to the heat of the sun.

His urgency communicated itself to her so that she didn't stop him when he slid his hands beneath the thin wrapper, seeking the softness of her rounded body. But as though her very acquiescence made him aware of his responsibilities in all this, he uttered a shuddering protest, and dragging her arms from around his neck he thrust himself up and away from her.

'No, Sophie!' he ground out thickly. 'Not here. Not like this. We have to talk first.'

His words sobered her, and she was wrapping the folds of her gown closely about her when there was a knock at her door and without waiting for any summons her father and stepmother entered the room. They took in the picture of Sophie still lying on the bed and Robert standing by the uncurtained windows in one sweeping glance. Sophie sensed Laura's assessment of her flushed cheeks and Robert's unbuttoned shirt, and with a lithe movement slid off the bed, and said: 'It's all right, both of you. Robert hasn't seduced me.'

Doctor Kemble was the first to speak. 'Robert! Your mother has been telling me that you've broken your engagement to Emma. I've no need to ask if this is true, obviously.' His eyes swept them both again. 'What I do want to know is, what do you intend to do now?'

Robert hunched his shoulders. 'Didn't Mother tell you that, too?'

Doctor Kemble sighed impatiently. 'Yes. Yes, she said you intended to ask Sophie to marry you. Is that the truth?'

Sophie clasped her hands together, and her eyes

sought Robert's joyously. He gave her a small smile that enfolded them both in a small intimate relationship that no one else could share. Then he turned to her father.

'That's right,' he agreed evenly.

'And have you done so?'

'Not yet——'

'Then I wish you wouldn't.'

'*Daddy!*'

But Sophie's protest went ignored as Doctor Kemble continued to gaze at his stepson. 'You can't ask Sophie to marry you, Robert. Your duties are all towards Emma at this time. I haven't said anything before because she asked me not to, but Emma confided in me while she was here. She said she had the strongest suspicions that she was pregnant.'

CHAPTER NINE

CORFU airport was small but efficient, the road to Harriet Tarrant's villa narrow and lined with walled gardens and citrus groves. The villa itself was set up in the hills, classical in design, white-painted walls, cool arched doorways, grilled balconies, and black shutters that nailed back. The gardens were a riot of colour, there was a sun-dappled trellis where vines wound and grapes hung in luscious bunches, and a paved patio gave on to a swimming pool which would prove most inviting in the early morning or in the waning heat of late afternoon. Below the villa, the terraced hillside fell away to stark rocks above the greeny-blue waters of the Ionian Sea.

Sophie found her first few days at the villa taken up with getting used to her new surroundings. She met Nana and Spiro, Harriet's two research assistants, and learned a little of what was expected of her. She rose early and went to bed early, and the tablets her father had relented and given her assured her of a night's rest.

She supposed her parents and Simon were in Brittany at this time. It was the first holiday they had spent without her, but she supposed Vicky Page would not complain. Without her their numbers were even. Of Robert—and Emma—she tried not to think at all, but of course that was practically impossible...

She couldn't help but wonder what had happened since she left England two weeks ago. At that time, a week after her father's shattering announcement of Emma's condition, Robert had been grim and unapproachable, denying even a discussion of his possible fatherhood, beyond stating unequivocally that he would not be held responsible.

Sophie still felt sick when she recalled the horror of that awful night when her father had destroyed in one sentence everything she had dreamed and hoped for. No wonder Emma had been content to allow Robert his moment of freedom. She had known that sooner or later he would be tied to her with bands stronger than that of an engagement ring.

The worst part had been Robert's denunciation of Doctor Kemble's statement. For a moment Sophie had thought he would strike her father, so angry did he become, but then he had turned on her, demanding savagely whether she believed what her father had said.

Sophie had had to believe it. She knew her father would not deliberately tell lies to separate them. But when she had tried to tell Robert this he had released a flow of invective which had left her weak and shaking. Then, without waiting for her father to order him to leave, he had flung himself out of the bedroom and out of the house, driving away heaven knew where to expunge his frustration.

When he returned the following morning, he was pale but composed. He had packed his bags and told his mother he was leaving for the site at Cymtraeth. When he returned the following weekend, Sophie was ready to leave with Harriet Tarrant.

The work Sophie had to do for her employer was not arduous. On the contrary, she had plenty of time to enjoy the pool and the beauties of the countryside around them, and although she cried herself to sleep most nights, she managed to fill her days.

Harriet Tarrant seemed to enjoy her young employee's company. When they were not working at the mound of information and correspondence which had accrued in her absence, she often came to find Sophie and sat with her, talking to her, telling her about her early life with her late husband, who had been a mining engineer, and how she had first evinced the idea to write about Greek mythology. Sophie didn't talk much about herself beyond the usual biographies of her parents and stepbrothers, but her expressive voice revealed more than she was aware.

Towards the end of her second week at the villa, she received a letter from her stepmother.

On her arrival Sophie had written a formal little letter of notification to her parents, advising them of her journey and assuring them of her well-being. Since then she had had no contact with them at all, and consequently she felt no particular sense of apprehension when she slit open the envelope. But what she read quickly wiped what little colour she had from her already pale cheeks and Harriet Tarrant, sitting at her desk a few feet away, watched her expression with increasing concern. Sophie uttered a little cry of protest, and the hand holding the letter fell limply to her side. With an exclamation, Harriet pushed back her chair and went to her, putting an arm about her shaking shoulders, and saying: 'What is it, Sophie? What is it, my dear? You're as white as a sheet! Come and sit down.'

Sophie shook her head vigorously. 'I—I'm all right, Mrs. Tarrant. It—it's my—my stepbrother. He—he's in hospital!'

Harriet looked down at the letter. 'May I read it?' she asked quietly, and with a helpless gesture Sophie thrust the letter into her hand, going to stand by the wide arched doors which stood wide to the patio, her palms pressed painfully to her cheeks.

Harriet read the letter quickly. She couldn't help

but think that Laura Kemble had spared her stepdaughter nothing. Sophie's stepbrother, Robert, had had an accident at the building site at Cymtraeth. He was in hospital now with severe facial and head injuries, fractured ribs, and multiple cuts and bruises.

Harriet swung round on the girl compassionately, shaking her head. 'Oh, Sophie!' she exclaimed. 'What a terrible thing to happen! I suppose you'd like leave of absence to go home and see him, wouldn't you?'

Sophie shook her head again. 'No.'

'No?' Harriet looked again at the letter. Then with raised eyebrows she made a confused gesture. 'But—I should have thought——'

'Robert doesn't need me. If you read on you'll see that—that Emma, his fiancée, is staying at Penn Warren.'

Harriet skimmed the latter few lines of the letter. 'So what? You're his stepsister. You have a right to be there.'

'No.' Sophie gulped. 'I don't want to go.'

Harriet stared at her penetratingly. 'You know, Sophie, I don't believe you.' She paused. 'Oh, I know I don't know you very well yet, but you strike me as the kind of young woman who would care about her family.'

Sophie strove for composure. 'Of course I care about them. I—I'm very upset about Robert, naturally. I—I just don't see what I can do.'

'And don't you think your parents—particularly your stepmother—would welcome your presence right now? Good heavens, Sophie, there are bound to be things you can do. And besides, I'm sure your stepbrother would like to see another familiar face——'

'No!' Sophie pressed her hands over her ears. 'No, no, no! Don't ask me! Please—don't ask me!' And to her complete ignominy and disgrace, she collapsed into tears.

Harriet let her cry for a while, and then she drew the girl's hands determinedly aside, and dried her eyes. 'Now,' she said. 'Suppose you tell me how long you've been in love with this stepbrother of yours, hmm?'

It was such a relief to tell somebody, to spill all the pain and humiliation she had suffered and been unable to share with anyone else. They had all been involved—her stepmother and brother, her father, even John Meredith had not been objective. But Harriet Tarrant was, and her verdict was surprisingly sympathetic.

'So this—Emma is back at the house, is she?' she observed thoughtfully. 'And naturally you think the engagement is back on.'

'It *has* to be!'

'Why does it?'

Sophie stared at her aghast. 'You can ask that?'

'Of course. Even supposing Emma is pregnant, even supposing it is Robert's child, there's no law which states that he has to marry her.'

'But—but he must!'

'Why? Lots of men in his position haven't.'

'But—but——' Sophie faltered. 'Robert's not like that.'

'What is he like?'

Sophie sniffed. 'He's—he's an honourable man.'

'You think so?'

'Of course.'

'Then do you think this honourable man would bow out of his responsibilities as you're accusing him of doing?'

'I don't understand.'

'Sophie, you told me that Robert stated that the child could not be his.'

'Yes.'

'Do you think an honourable man would do that? If the child was his, I mean?'

Sophie was confused. She rose from the chair into which Harriet had pressed her and walked restlessly about the room. 'I don't know.'

'Precisely. So there's the possibility that it's not his child.'

'But whose else could it be?'

'Perhaps there is no child,' remarked Harriet quietly.

Sophie swallowed convulsively. 'No—child?' she echoed. 'But my father's a doctor. He—he would know.'

'Did he examine her?'

'I don't know. I—I don't think so.'

'So. We only have Emma's word that she is pregnant.'

'But—but she wouldn't dare——'

'Why wouldn't she?'

'Someone would find out.'

'It might have been a calculated risk. Men are notoriously jealous of their masculinity. To question such an eventuality is like questioning their own impotency. And you did say that Emma was Robert's mistress, didn't you?'

'Emma lived with him, yes.'

'She told you that?'

'Does it matter?'

'It might.'

Sophie sighed. 'Oh, yes, I think she did. Anyway, people do, don't they? And—and Robert said he—he had—used her.'

Harriet sucked her cheeks in thoughtfully. 'Nevertheless, it's all supposition, can't you see that? If she's not pregnant, Emma has been a very clever girl, hasn't she? She must have guessed that Robert was cooling off, if indeed he was ever that keen. It was a master stroke to confide in your father. She would know that he would never permit you to get involved with Robert if there was any question of her being pregnant.'

Sophie twisted her hands together. 'Oh, Mrs. Tarrant, what if you're right?'

'If I am, you've done that stepbrother of yours a terrible injustice.'

'And—and now he's had this—this accident.'

Harriet reached for a cigarette. 'Accident, yes. Are you going to see him?'

'Do—do *you* think I should?'

'Oh, no, Sophie.' Harriet inhaled deeply on her cigarette. 'You must make your own decisions.'

'Of course I *want* to see him!' Sophie chewed at her lower lip. 'Oh, God, what if his injuries are fatal!'

'I think if they were, your stepmother would have phrased her letter a little less brutally.'

Sophie looked at the older woman quickly. 'Yes. Yes, perhaps you're right.'

'Go, then. Talk to this Emma, decide for yourself whether you think she's pregnant——'

'I'd be biased.'

'Then you'll have to try and be objective, won't you? Go and see Robert, talk to him. Always providing he's prepared to talk to you.' She sighed impatiently as her words made Sophie wince. 'Sophie, you may have been jumping to conclusions, you have to accept that. But, if the girl is pregnant ...' she paused and Sophie felt the familiar despair she always felt at the images this evoked, '—if she is pregnant, you must consider carefully before making any judgement. If you really love Robert, you may find you're prepared to forgive him.'

Sophie was shocked. 'You—you mean you think I should allow him to decide what he wants to do?' she exclaimed incredulously.

Harriet's lips twisted. 'Sex is a curious thing, Sophie. It can be the ultimate consummation of a man and woman's love for one another—or simply the satisfaction of a desperate human need. If the latter circumstances apply, it's up to both participants to ensure that no life evolves from such a union. But if by some freak mischance it does, do you think that is sufficient reason for a man to marry a woman he doesn't love? Who benefits from such a liaison? Not the man, probably not the woman, and certainly not the child.'

Sophie made a bemused gesture. 'If my father could hear what you're saying!'

'He wouldn't approve?' And as Sophie shook her head: 'He's living in the past. Thank goodness, people are becoming less rigid in their attitudes towards circumstances such as we have been discussing. Marriages are not all made in heaven—a large percentage of them are made in hell, and no one should be forced to sacrifice his life because of one mistake.'

Sophie digested this slowly. 'But they were—engaged,' she pointed out honestly.

'I agree, it's difficult. But Emma, I imagine, went into this with her eyes open. I have no doubt she'll come out of it the same way. She sounds a very self-sufficient young woman to me. Do you believe Robert would take the chance of something like this happening if he wasn't sure he wanted to marry her?'

Sophie spread her hands helplessly. 'I—I don't know what to think.'

'Then I suggest you start thinking about Robert. He may not be dying, Sophie, but his injuries sound serious enough to me. Have you considered how you might feel if he was permanently maimed—or blinded?'

'Oh, don't—*don't*!' Sophie put her hands over her eyes.

'Does it appal you?'

'Yes. *Yes!*'

'Then perhaps you'd better stay away.'

'No!' Sophie's hands fell to her sides, balling into fists. 'Do you think I care what his injuries are—for myself? I only care for him! Whatever the outcome, I shan't change.'

Harriet gave a wry smile. 'I must be getting foolish in my old age. I think I've just talked myself out of the best assistant I've ever had.'

Sophie looked at her steadily. 'If—if things don't work out—can I come back?'

Harriet turned away to stub out her cigarette. 'I don't think you need to ask that question, Sophie,' she said.

Sophie arrived back at Penn Warren three days later.

Although she had telegraphed the date and estimated time of her arrival, she was not surprised when there was no one to meet her at London Airport. She took a taxi into the city and caught a train from Paddington, but when she walked along the platform at Hereford and found there was no one waiting there for her either, a certain tightness invaded her throat. She walked quickly out of the station, and virtually collided with Simon. She stared up at him silently, tears trembling on her lashes, and with an exclamation he pulled her into his arms. 'Okay, Sophie,' he said quietly. 'I'm here.'

The station wagon was waiting in the parking area and Simon gently guided her towards it, settling her in the front and stowing her suitcases on the back seat. Then he slid in beside her, started the engine, and drove away without asking any unnecessary questions.

Sophie stole a grateful glance at his familiar profile. It was good to know that in spite of everything, Simon had not deserted her.

Swallowing her pride, she said: 'How—how is he, Simon? Is he very badly hurt? How did it happen?'

Simon negotiated a set of traffic lights and then sighed. 'What did my mother write you?'

'Oh, she said he had head and facial injuries, broken bones—I don't remember it word for word. Did it happen on the building site?'

'Yes,' Simon added.

'But how? Don't they wear helmets or something?'

'Yes. Usually they do.'

'Well, then?'

Simon's fingers tightened round the wheel. 'For some reason, Rob wasn't wearing his. He walked straight into the path of a girder. It was lucky he wasn't killed outright.'

'Oh, no!' Sophie's voice quivered.

'I'm afraid so.' Simon glanced at her. 'It was a crazy thing to do.'

'But why? Why did he do it?'

'You're implying that he did it on purpose?'

Sophie shook her head. 'I don't know what to think.'

'Well, it occurred to me at the time. Particularly— particularly in the circumstances.'

'Oh, Simon!' Sophie's hands clenched round the strap of her handbag. 'And his injuries? How bad are they?'

'Bad enough.' Simon spoke emotionlessly. 'At first they thought he had a fractured skull, but it appears now it was only severe concussion. His face is a mess, I warn you. The steel tore his cheek half off.' Sophie closed her eyes in horror, and he went on, deliberately removing all expression from his voice, 'He was knocked to the ground from about twenty feet up. He broke a couple of ribs, tore his legs in a couple of places. He has bruises everywhere.'

'Oh, God!' Sophie opened her eyes again. 'And when did this happen? Your mother gave no details.'

'Ten days ago——'

'*Ten days!*' Sophie gasped. 'But I only got your mother's letter three days ago. Couldn't she—couldn't anybody—have cabled me?'

Simon concentrated on the road ahead. 'Mother's taken this badly,' he replied. 'I'm afraid, to a certain extent, she blames you.'

'Blames me?' Sophie nodded. 'I see. I suppose she has that right.'

'Emma's at the house, you know. She's been staying in Caernarvon with my mother, but Robert refused to see her, so your father suggested she came and stayed with us.'

Sophie blinked. 'Caernarvon?' Then she gulped. 'You mean Robert is in hospital in Caernarvon?'

'Of course. Didn't you know?'

'No.' Sophie slumped. 'I suppose I just thought he'd be in Hereford. Oh, how stupid of me! I never considered how ludicrous that would be.' She stared blindly out of the car window. *Robert, Robert,* she murmured under her breath. Miles and miles away at Caernarvon. When would she get to see him? When would she be *allowed* to see him?

She turned eagerly to Simon. 'Will you drive me to Caernarvon?'

Simon glanced at her. 'When? Not tonight, that's for sure.'

'Then when? Tomorrow morning?'

Simon shook his head. 'That rather depends on your father, doesn't it? He wanted to telegraph you to remain in Corfu. I persuaded him that naturally you'd want to come home.'

'Thank you, Simon.'

'But going to Caernarvon—I don't know.'

'But I've got to go, don't you see? I—I must see Robert.'

'Why? Nothing's changed.'

'What do you mean?'

Simon's mouth turned down at the corners. 'Emma is pregnant. She had it confirmed two weeks ago.'

Sophie pressed a hand to her stomach as a sharp pain shot through her. 'Who confirmed it? Has Daddy examined her?'

'Of course not. Sophie, everything has gone haywire these past two weeks. Don't you realise, this was supposed to be the beginning of our holiday in Brittany?'

'I know.'

'Well then, you must appreciate that all our arrangements have had to be cancelled. There's been no time to question something that's already a *fait accompli*.'

Sophie took a deep breath. 'And Robert still denies that the child is his?'

'Sophie, Robert has been in no fit state to admit or deny anything.'

'But you said he had refused to see her.'

'He's refused to see anybody. Even his mother.'

'What?'

'It's the truth. Oh, she's staying in Caernarvon to be near the hospital, but apart from when he was unconscious she hasn't seen him.'

Sophie was aghast. 'But why?'

Simon shrugged. 'Your guess is as good as mine.'

'Don't you have any idea?'

Simon's face hardened. 'Oh, yes, I have ideas.' He paused. 'But you might not like to hear them.'

'Go on—please.'

'All right. I think you're to blame. I suspect Rob

didn't much care what happened to him after you ran off to Corfu. I think he intended to—do himself an injury.'

'Simon!'

'You asked me to tell you,' he reminded her quietly. 'Now he finds he hasn't succeeded. And what's more, he's scarred for life.'

'But, Simon, what could I do? You said yourself that Robert and I—well, that the parents would never agree.'

Simon heaved a heavy sigh. 'I know I did. But you must have known I had my own selfish reasons for wanting you to believe me. Do you think I'm not aware of my own culpability?'

'Then don't you see that it's imperative that I do see Robert?'

'He may refuse to see you, too.'

'Nevertheless, I have to try.'

Simon made a dismissing movement of his shoulders. 'I suggest you talk it over with your father this evening. You're not eighteen yet, you know.'

It was early evening when they turned between the gates of Penn Warren, and when the car stopped on the drive Sophie's father came out to meet them. He looked a little more strained than usual, but his welcome was reassuringly warm.

'So you came, Sophie,' he murmured, after embracing her. 'I can't say I'm sorry. No doubt Simon's told you that I wanted to stop you from rushing back, but now you're here ...' He smiled. 'I've missed you,' he finished simply.

Sophie's worst moment came when they entered the lounge and found Emma sitting smugly in an armchair by the window, knitting. She produced her usual insincere smile, and getting up made a great show of shaking hands. 'It's good to see you again, Sophie,' she said. Then she produced her handkerchief and blew her nose. 'Not that any of us would wish to meet in these circumstances, if we had the choice.'

Sophie glanced disbelievingly at her father, but he seemed not to have noticed anything affected about Emma's behaviour. On the contrary, he was smiling sympathetically at her, nodding at the truth in what she had said.

Sophie turned to Simon as a last resort, but his face was blank, and with a faint shrug, she said: 'No indeed. It's a terrible affair.'

Emma subsided into her chair again, apparently engulfed in grief, and Doctor Kemble moved towards the door. 'You must be hungry, Sophie. What would you like to eat?'

'Oh, nothing, thank you. I had a meal on the train,' lied Sophie, knowing herself incapable of eating a thing.

'Some coffee, then.'

'I'll make it.' Sophie took off the jacket of the cream suit she had worn to travel in. 'You sit down, Daddy. You look tired. I won't be long.'

It was a relief to escape to the kitchen, to the familiar chores attached to making coffee. But her relief was short-lived when the door opened a few minutes later and Emma came in.

'Can I give you a hand?' she asked, in a voice loud enough to be heard in the lounge.

'I can manage, thanks.' Sophie poured the coffee grounds into the filter.

Emma did not take the hint. 'I'll get the cups,' she insisted smoothly.

As she was setting out the cups and saucers on the tray, Emma cast a speculative look in Sophie's direction. 'I suppose Simon has told you the good news?' she suggested.

Sophie had known this was bound to come sooner or later, but she was still unprepared for the raw shock it still gave her. 'What news?' she temporised.

'About the baby, of course.' Emma's lips tightened ever so slightly. 'The wedding has had to be brought forward, of course. Your stepmother's suggestion, I might add. Naturally, Robbie's accident has delayed things.'

Sophie squared her shoulders and turned to face the other girl. 'Yes, I knew about the baby,' she admitted tautly.

Emma smiled complacently. 'You'll be its aunt. Won't that be nice?'

'Don't you think we ought to wait until Robert's on his feet again before anticipating the event?' Sophie couldn't prevent the admonition bursting from her lips.

Emma patted her stomach insinuatively. 'I can't wait all that long.'

Sophie turned away. 'I understand Robert has refused to see you.'

'He's refused to see anyone,' retorted Emma coldly.

Sophie's fingers curled over the formica surface of a bench unit. 'I want to see him.'

'He won't see you!' Emma sneered. 'He blames you for what happened.'

Sophie's nails dug into her palms. 'Nevertheless, I want to see him.'

'You're wasting your time.'

'I'll be the judge of that.'

'Do you think your father—or your stepmother, for that matter—will permit you to upset him again?'

'I didn't upset him——'

'Yes, you did. Before you came home, we had no problems. The engagement—the coming wedding—we were happy, really happy. Then you came along and tried to ruin it all!'

'I—don't—believe—that,' Sophie got out tautly.

'You don't want to believe it. It tears you to pieces that someone else—some other girl—has the right to demand his undivided attention, doesn't it? You're jealous, that's all. Jealous of what we have—what we've been to one another!'

Sophie had to restrain the impulse to scream at Emma, scream that she was right, she was jealous, but that it wasn't true about their being happy together. Or was it? She had only heard one side of it, after all. But Robert couldn't have been lying, he couldn't!

To her relief the percolator switched itself off at that moment, enabling her to unplug it and stand it on the tray. Then she asked Emma if she would open the door, and carried the tray through to the lounge.

Although Sophie was eager to talk to her father about Robert, she decided it would be easier to do so alone. As it was, she had to listen to a general discussion of Robert's condition, schooling her features not to reveal the desperation she was feeling.

Later Emma went to wash up the dirty cups and saucers and realising that Sophie wanted to speak to her father, Simon left them alone. Immediately Sophie left her seat to sit on the arm of her father's chair.

'Daddy,' she murmured, without prevarication, 'I want to go and see Robert tomorrow.'

Doctor Kemble looked up at her anxiously. 'I don't think that's a very good idea, Sophie. Besides, Robert is not seeing anyone.'

'I know that. But I want to try.'

'Why?'

'Why? *Why?* You can ask me that!'

Her father bent his head to fill his pipe. 'What do you hope to achieve?'

'I love Robert, Daddy. And—and he loves me.'

There was silence for a few moments and then Doctor Kemble said quietly: 'Were I to accept that that were so, I would still be against you going to see him.'

Sophie's shoulders sagged. 'Oh, Daddy!'

'Sophie, be sensible about this! Whether he likes it or not, Robert is as successfully bound to Emma as he would be had he already put a wedding ring on her finger.'

'We only have Emma's word that she's pregnant!' stated Sophie bitterly.

Her father snorted. 'Sophie! What are you suggesting? What possible reason could Emma have had for confiding in me if she was not expecting a baby? Good heavens, at that time there was no question of a split between her and Robert!'

'Wasn't there?'

'What do you mean?'

'Oh, Daddy, a woman knows when a man—— Oh, Emma must have guessed!'

'I don't want to hear another word!' Doctor Kemble looked angrily at his daughter. 'This whole affair has got completely out of hand. You will please me by not mentioning it again.'

Sophie shook her head, her lips trembling a little. 'Am I not to be permitted to see Robert, then?'

There was another significant silence, and then Doctor Kemble expelled a heavy sigh. 'I don't suppose I can actually forbid you to go to Caernarvon. But bear in mind, he has every likelihood of refusing to see you either.'

'Does that mean I can go?'

'Go? Go where?'

Emma's questioning voice broke into their conversation, and Sophie's stomach muscles tightened as she wondered how long the other girl had been listening.

'Er—Sophie is going to see Robert,' said Doctor Kemble quickly.

'Oh, is she?' Emma hid her irritation. 'When?'

Doctor Kemble looked at his daughter again. 'I don't know. Sophie?'

Sophie slid off the arm of his chair. 'Tomorrow,' she said defiantly. 'Simon said he would drive me.'

'Then I'll come, too. If I may.' Emma was very confident.

Sophie's father hesitated, looking at each of them in turn. 'I—yes. Why not?'

Sophie's facial muscles felt paralysed, but she managed to make some sort of comment and then excused herself to do her unpacking. So Emma was coming to Caernarvon with them. So what? That didn't change anything.

CHAPTER TEN

THE Hospital of St. Theresa stood in its own grounds not far from the city centre. Recent extensions had given it a partially prefabricated appearance, but the main buildings were reassuringly red-brick and hung with ivy. It was early afternoon when they arrived, Simon having insisted upon stopping en route for lunch, although none of them had been hungry, and the strain on Sophie's nerves had left her looking pale and drawn.

Laura Kemble met them in the reception area, disapproval of Sophie's presence evident in every look she cast in her stepdaughter's direction. She made a great fuss of welcoming Emma, enquiring after her health, showing that she had no intention of changing her opinion because of what had happened.

'How is he?' Sophie had to ask, but Laura looked at Simon as she replied.

'He's stronger. As a matter of fact, I did get to speak to him late yesterday afternoon, but he's still so sensitive about his appearance that I can't get through to him.'

'Are you sure that's all it is?' suggested Simon quietly, and his mother uttered an impatient ejaculation.

'Don't you start, Simon!' she declared unsteadily. 'Don't you think I have enough to worry about?'

'Sophie wants to see him,' said Simon, by way of a reply. 'Who does she need to see to get permission?'

'I doubt very much whether the doctors will admit her,' retorted Laura. 'She's not a blood relative, is she?'

Sophie gasped, and Simon put his arm about her, pushing her towards the lifts. 'I know the way, Sophie,' he said, glaring at his mother. 'I've no doubt the Sister on Rob's ward will be able to help us.'

'Wait!' Emma, who had said little up to the present, moved towards them. 'We'll all come up with you. Robert will decide who he wants to see anyway.'

Robert's room was on the fourth floor. He had been in the intensive care unit initially, Simon explained, as they travelled up, but now he had a room of his own. There was an antiseptic smell about the hospital which invaded Sophie's nostrils and caused a churning sense of apprehension in her stomach. Until this moment Robert's condition had been a distant thing, almost an impersonal thing, but here, surrounded by the sights and sounds of the busy hospital, she became fully aware of the seriousness of what it involved.

Sister Mallory was a woman in her early forties, cool and efficient, conscious of her position without being over-confident. She greeted Laura politely, said hello to Emma and Simon, and then looked questioningly at Sophie.

'Er—this—this is my stepdaughter,' said Laura with reluctance. 'She's been working in Greece, but she's flown home to—to enquire about Robert.'

'She's flown home to *see* Robert,' amended Simon impatiently. 'Is that possible?'

'I—I'd like to see my fiancé, too,' put in Emma, successfully conveying the impression that while she did not want to intrude, she did have certain privileges over the other girl.

They were all gathered in Sister Mallory's small office, and with a gesture she indicated that they should be seated. Then, with a withdrawn smile, she faced them across her desk.

'Mrs. Kemble, you must know that Mr. Ydris has

refused to see any of his family. Even you.'

'I spoke to him yesterday afternoon,' said Laura quickly.

'I know you did.' Sister Mallory sighed. 'But that was at your insistence, and afterwards—afterwards Mr. Ydris adjured me not to admit you again.'

Laura sat back aghast, and Sophie felt terribly sorry for her. Even Simon leant across and pressed his mother's hand, and she held on to him like a lifeline.

'I'm sorry.' Sister Mallory was obviously ill at ease having to convey such information. 'However, I can tell you that your son is improving, Mrs. Kemble. We should be able to remove the plaster from his ribs in a week's time, and his cuts and bruises are improving rapidly. As for his cheek—the stitches will be staying in for a little longer and later, when he's fully recovered, we'll be able to do some skin grafts.'

'Skin grafts!' Laura pressed a handkerchief to her lips. 'Is it that bad?'

'You know how bad it is, Mrs. Kemble,' replied Sister Mallory quietly. 'But you must remember, it could have been a lot worse. There could have been brain damage . . .'

'I know, I know.' Laura shook her head bitterly, and Sophie moved to the edge of her chair.

'Please,' she said, attracting all eyes suddenly, 'couldn't you ask—ask my stepbrother whether he—whether he would see me?'

Sister Mallory frowned, but Laura turned on her stepdaughter. 'How can you suggest such a thing, Sophie! Don't you have any shame, any pity? If it wasn't for you, none of this might have happened!'

Sophie flinched at the contempt in Laura's eyes, and Sister Mallory, sensing a family quarrel, shook her head. 'He's sleeping at the moment, Miss Kemble. I couldn't disturb him. But I'll mention your name when he wakes up, if you'd like me to.'

'Oh—yes—no—that is, it doesn't matter.' Sophie curled herself into the smallest position possible. 'Forget it.'

Outside again, the air was blessedly cool. Laura looked more strained than ever, but Sophie thought that Emma could hardly hide her jubilation at Sophie's letdown. However, she hid it well when Laura turned to her and said: 'Are you driving back tonight, Emma?'

'What else is there for me to do?' Emma made it sound apathetic.

Laura hesitated. 'I thought you might like to stay at my hotel overnight. Driving so far in your condition in one day can't be good for you.'

'Oh, yes. I see.' Emma glanced triumphantly at the others. 'Well, naturally I'd love to stay. But how would I get back tomorrow?'

'I've no doubt Simon could come back for you, couldn't you, Simon?' Laura turned to her son, and at his indifferent nod, inclined her head. 'There you are. It's all arranged. I'll be glad of your company.'

Emma was eager to grasp at any tenuous link with Robert, and Sophie and Simon left them to walk to their hotel a few yards from the hospital grounds. Once in Simon's car, however, Sophie stopped him from starting the engine.

'I'm going back,' she said distinctly. 'Not now. Not at this minute. But later—after tea.'

Simon expelled his breath on a whistle. 'I see.'

'Will you wait for me?'

'Do I have any choice?'

'Of course. I can catch a train—I'm not helpless.'

'After tea? I think not.'

'Then I'll stay overnight. I have a little money——'

'Forget it.' Simon hunched his shoulders. 'I'll wait.'

Sophie looked at him gratefully. 'You've changed, Simon, do you know that?'

Simon snorted. 'Let's say I know when I'm licked,' he commented wryly.

Sister Mallory had gone off duty by the time Sophie returned to the fourth floor of the hospital and in her place was a younger woman, Sister Evans. When Sophie explained who she was, Sister Evans shook her head regretfully.

'I'm afraid Mr. Ydris doesn't have visitors,' she said.

Sophie stifled her frustration. 'Couldn't you just ask him? Tell him who I am?'

Sister Evans shook her head. 'That's more than my job is worth, Miss Kemble. It's Doctor Francis you need to see.'

Sophie spread her hands. 'So where is Doctor Francis?'

'I'm afraid he's off duty, Miss Kemble.'

Sophie felt tears welling up behind her eyes. 'Couldn't I see him, then? Isn't there somewhere I could go and just look at him? Through a window or something?'

Sister Evans hesitated. 'You could—look through the panes in his door, I suppose,' she murmured doubtfully. 'But you'd have to be quiet.'

'Oh, I would!' Sophie clenched her fists.

'Very well, Miss Kemble. Come this way.'

They walked further along the aseptically white corridor until Sister Evans paused outside a cream panelled door.

'This is Mr. Ydris's room, Miss Kemble,' she whispered. 'If you look through there...'

Sophie peered through the tinted panes of glass near the top of the door. Beyond was a cell-like room, stark and clinical, a narrow iron-posted bed occupying the centre of the floor. And in the bed a man was lying, propped up on pillows, spasmodically turning the pages of a magazine. Above the opened jacket of his pyjamas she could see the white line of his plaster cast, there were elastic plasters covering parts of his hands, but it was to his face that her eyes were drawn. The left half of his face was pale and showed the marks of scratches that were steadily disappearing, but his right cheek had been partially torn away, and an ugly line of stitches gave what was left a patchwork appearance.

'Oh, God! *Robert!*' Her heart went out to him in a wave of love and longing. Involuntarily she took a step forward, and her foot accidentally caught the door and set it shuddering.

Immediately Robert looked up. 'Who is it? Who's there?' he demanded, and with an impatient look at Sophie, Sister Evans entered the room.

'It's only me, Mr. Ydris,' she said, giving her professional smile. 'How are you feeling this evening?'

Robert stared at her penetratingly. 'I thought I heard voices. Who's out there?'

'No one, Mr. Ydris——'

'It's me, Robert!' Sophie could bear the suspense no longer and ignoring Sister Evans' automatic reproof she advanced towards the bed. 'Hello, Robert. How are you?'

There was a moment's complete silence while Robert stared at her grimly, and then Sister Evans made a helpless gesture. 'I'm sorry, Mr. Ydris. Miss Kemble persuaded me to show her your room. She promised she wouldn't attempt to talk to you.'

Robert returned his attention to the magazine in his hands. 'That's all right, Sister Evans. You can go. I'll speak to—to Miss Kemble.'

'You will?' Sister Evans didn't know whether to feel glad or sorry. 'Very well, Mr. Ydris. I'll give you ten minutes.'

The door swung to behind her and Sophie put **out** her hands appealingly. 'Oh, Robert, Robert! What have you done to yourself?'

She went down on her knees beside the bed and sought his fingers with hers, but he avoided her touch, concentrating still on the magazine. 'I don't know why you've come here, Sophie,' he said coldly. 'I didn't ask to see you.'

'But I wanted to see you!' she exclaimed. 'I had to see you!'

'Why? I'm alive. I'm not at death's door. You had no neeed to come all this way just to find that out.'

'I didn't come just to find that out,' she protested tremulously. 'Robert, you have no idea how I felt when—when I received your mother's letter.'

'Revolted, I should think.'

'What do you mean?'

Robert looked up then, giving her the full benefit of his scarred countenance. 'Well, I'm not a pretty sight, am I?'

Sophie shook her head impatiently. 'I don't care what you look like!'

'No?' Robert looked down at the magazine again. 'No, I don't suppose you do. Whatever I look like, you won't have to see too much of me.'

'Robert, stop it!'

He looked up again. 'Stop it? Stop what?'

'Stop saying such—such horrible things.'

'They're not horrible things. They're the truth. Why pretend? You're working in Corfu, and eventually no doubt, you'll go on to university. And providing the company don't sack me for negligence, my next assignment is in Canada.'

'*Canada!*' Sophie pressed her palms together. 'Will—will Emma be going with you?'

'Emma?' Robert's mouth hardened. 'No.'

'But—you'll be married by then.'

'I have no intention of marrying Emma,' stated Robert bleakly. 'And now, if you've nothing more to say——'

'But I have!' Sophie sprang to her feet, looking down at him desperately, trying to still the palpitations of her heart. 'But—if she's pregnant...'

Robert regarded her with dislike. 'Go away, Sophie. We have nothing more to say to one another.'

'But we have, we have!' Sophie took a deep breath. 'Robert, that night at—at Penn Warren; you were going to ask me to marry you, weren't you?'

'I don't wish to discuss it.'

'Robert, *please*!' Her tone was entreating and his eyes narrowed.

'Well?'

'Well, I—I will marry you. If—if you still want me.'

'Are you crazy?' Robert's face twisted. 'My God, what is this? You're telling me you'll marry me even though you believe Emma is expecting my child?'

'I don't know what to believe. We only have Emma's word——'

'It was good enough for you before,' he snapped bitterly.

'It wasn't like that. Robert, my father——'

'Your father doesn't govern your thoughts. You believed him. Just as you still believe him, deep inside. I wonder what he would say if he could hear you now?'

'I don't care what he would say——'

'No more do I. I don't care what you say either, Sophie. Just go away and leave me alone. I can do without any of you.'

How Sophie reached the car again, she never knew. She was shaking so much her teeth were chattering and Simon left her to go into an off-licence and buy a small bottle of brandy which he opened and insisted on her drinking from. The raw spirit was warming; it made her choke and cough, but at least it banished the icy coldness which seemed to have entered her veins.

Realising they could not go on sitting in the hospital car-park indefinitely, Simon eventually started the car and drove towards the exit. But as they were going out, two women were coming in, and one of them stumbled in her haste to avoid the car and fell, hitting her head against the brick wall.

'Lord, it's Emma!' exclaimed Simon, stopping and leaping out of the car. 'Hell, have I killed her?'

The shock of the accident brought Sophie to life. She, too, jumped out of the car and ran to where Simon and his mother were kneeling by Emma's still body. 'Is she all right?'

Laura looked up at her stepdaughter angrily. 'It's no thanks to you if she is!' she snapped. 'For heaven's sake, Simon, can't you see she's been knocked unconscious? Go and get someone, a nurse or a doctor. She needs examining to make sure she hasn't damaged herself.'

Simon shrugged helplessly at Sophie and ran off, while Sophie wetted her handkerchief and dabbed at the bruising on Emma's forehead. 'Whatever happened?' she asked, looking at her stepmother. 'She acted as if Simon was about to run her down.'

Laura looked as though she was going to refuse to speak to her stepdaughter, and then she muttered something non-committal. 'I think she recognised you, if you must know,' she replied curtly. 'I expect she wondered what you were doing here. As I am wondering now.'

'I—I had to see Robert,' said Sophie quietly. 'And I did.'

'What did he say?' Laura couldn't hide her interest

174

now, but Emma was stirring and Sophie's reply was postponed.

'Oh, what happened?' Emma tried to struggle up on to her elbows.

Laura soothed her gently. 'You tripped, my dear, and hit your head. How do you feel?'

Emma licked her dry lips, her eyes flickering over Sophie and showing her surprise. 'I—I've got a bit of a headache, that's all.'

Laura glanced towards the lighted entrance of the hospital. 'Well, don't worry. I've sent Simon for help.' She tried to make light of it. 'An ideal place to have an accident—practically on the steps of the hospital!'

But Emma seemed agitated now. 'I'm all right, really I am,' she exclaimed, struggling to get up against their restraining hands. 'I don't need help. I'm fine!'

'Nonsense.' Laura was adamant. 'There's no point in taking any chances when there's no need to do so. I shan't be content until you've had a thorough examination.'

'No——'

Sophie could see Simon coming now. There were two men with him, one in a porter's uniform, and the other obviously a houseman. She looked down at Emma. 'It's too late,' she said. 'Here's Simon.'

Emma was carried into Casualty on a stretcher and Sophie, Simon and Laura waited in Outpatients for her to emerge. Sophie couldn't help recollecting Emma's agitation and the possible reasons for it. What if she was not pregnant? Would anyone find out? Was that what was troubling her? Surely she had no need to worry about that. At this early stage, it would be difficult to deny without thorough testing. And yet...

Turning to Simon, she said, 'Did you notice how upset Emma appeared to be?'

Simon nodded. 'I wonder why.'

'She could be concerned about losing—the baby.'

'*If* there is a baby.'

'Oh, what are you two saying?' Laura overheard the tale end of their conversation. 'Of course Emma's expecting a baby. I've had two myself. I know the symptoms. A woman always knows.'

Laura was so adamant that the spring of doubt which had risen inside Sophie as quickly was doused. Instead she sat on the edge of her chair, waiting impatiently for Emma to be announced unharmed and thus enable herself and Simon to leave.

But Emma did not emerge. Instead the houseman who had examined her approached them.

'You're Miss Norton's relatives?' he asked.

'Not exactly,' admitted Laura. 'She—she's going to marry my son.'

'Is she?' The houseman nodded. 'Oh, well, I have to tell you that we're keeping her in overnight.'

'You are?' Laura's lips parted anxiously. 'Is something wrong? It's not the baby, is it?'

'The baby, Mrs. Kemble?' Sophie thought she would always remember the astonishment on the houseman's face. 'What baby?'

Laura flushed. 'My son—that is—Emma is—pregnant.'

The houseman considered the notes on the pad in front of him. Then he looked at Simon. 'You are Miss Norton's fiancé, Mr. Kemble?'

Simon shook his head. 'No. My brother.'

'I see.' The houseman looked troubled. 'Well, I don't know quite how to say this, but Miss Norton is not pregnant. On that I can reassure you.'

Laura collapsed on to one of the wooden seats that lined the outpatients' area. '*Not* pregnant?' she echoed disbelievingly.

'Not pregnant,' assured the houseman firmly. He glanced at Sophie and Simon, and then looked at Laura again. 'Obviously, you've—er—misunderstood your son's and Miss Norton's reasons for getting married, Mrs. Kemble.'

Sophie had to sit down, too. Her legs felt like jelly, and this news, far from reassuring her, had knocked all the wind out of her. Oh, God! what a fool she had been, what fools they had all been! But that was no excuse. They had believed Emma before Robert, and that was unforgivable.

Laura managed to look up. 'You are—sure?'

'Oh, yes, Mrs. Kemble. A medical examination was not needed to confirm that fact. There are—outward signs. You understand?'

Laura turned away, pressing her lips to the knuckles of one hand. Simon took command.

'You say—Miss Norton has to stay in overnight?'

'Oh! Oh, yes.' The houseman consulted his papers. 'Actually, I'm sure she's going to be all right. It was not a serious blow to the head. But Miss Norton herself seems—nervous—agitated. Sufficiently so for me to recommend a night's observation.'

'I see.' Simon bent and helped both his mother and Sophie to their feet. 'I think we understand now. Thank you.'

'Miss Norton will be free to leave any time after ten tomorrow morning, Mr. Kemble.'

'Then I suggest you tell her that,' replied Simon, with a tight smile, and escorted the two women out of the hospital without permitting them a backward glance.

'I think we could all do with a good night's sleep, don't you, Mother?' he asked, urging them towards the station wagon. 'In our own beds. At Penn Warren, hmm?' And mutely Laura agreed.

CHAPTER ELEVEN

SOPHIE sat on the side of the swimming pool, dangling her feet in the water. Looking down at the slenderness of her limbs, the bones which were revealed through the honey-gold skin, she wished she had not climbed on to Harriet Tarrant's bathroom scales that morning. Until then she had been able to convince herself that her loss of weight was negligible, but now she knew that this was not so. The reason her clothes, even tight-fitting jeans, were hanging on her was because she had lost over a stone since returning to Corfu less than a month ago.

She passed an impatient hand over her eyes. These past few days since Harriet had been away on business had dragged. She had nothing to occupy her time. She had completed the work Harriet had left for her within a couple of days of Harriet's departure, albeit working longer hours than her employer would have approved. Since then, she had wandered restlessly about the place, unable to rid her mind of the thoughts that plagued it.

To begin with, when she first returned to Corfu after that tortuous interview with Robert and the subsequent discovery of Emma's deception, she had felt numb, mentally paralysed, capable of only surface sensitivities. She had renewed her relationship with Harriet without explanation further than that Robert was going to be all right, and applied herself to her work automatically.

Harriet had been wonderful. She had behaved as though nothing momentous had happened, had asked no questions, when dozens must have been trembling on her tongue, and generally made Sophie feel that in some strange way she had come home.

Within such a warm and sympathetic atmosphere, Sophie's temporary retreat from reality could not last. As the days went by, and the ice which seemed to have encased her heart melted, reaction of a different kind set in. Of course, she had had to confess the truth of what really happened on her visit to Conwynneth, and Harriet, for once, had had nothing constructive to say.

And so that awful week had stretched into two, and then three ... Sophie was often aware of Harriet watching her in those early days, but her understanding of the situation was such that Sophie felt no need to hide her feelings.

Nevertheless, while the mind was capable of absorbing a tremendous amount of pain, the body was less resilient. Although Sophie tried to eat the food Harriet's cook so painstakingly prepared for her, her appetite was practically non-existent, and she had found she could live on next to nothing. But living was one thing, remaining healthy was another. The combined strains of her existence were stripping the flesh from her body.

With an exclamation almost of self-disgust Sophie plunged into the cooling waters of the pool. If she had lived a hundred years before, she thought impatiently, she would have been said to be pining away. Was she, an emancipated female of the twentieth century, to allow such a thing to happen? Time would heal all things. Already the words Robert had said to her could be relived without too much agony. If the spirit could take it, why must the flesh be so weak? An old Spanish proverb she had once read sprang to her mind: *Take what you want, said God*, it had said, *take it—and pay for it*. Well, she was paying now for the things she had taken for granted.

She lunched alone on the patio and then sought the coolness of her room in the heat of the day. Although she never slept at this time she could not stand too much heat at the moment. She was a prey to headaches which she realised were the result of too little sustenance.

She had been lying there perhaps an hour when she heard the sound of a car droning up the hill to the villa and relief swept over her. Harriet was home! Thank heavens for that.

She slid off the bed and quickly dressed in a lemon cotton halter top and a short swinging cotton skirt. She stepped into thonged sandals and brushing carelessly at her hair hurried out through the wide entrance hall to where Harriet's car was drawing to a halt on the forecourt.

'Oh, am I glad to see you——' she was beginning as Harriet stepped out of the car, and then halted abruptly when her father also emerged. '*Daddy!*' Her eyes darted from one to the other of them. She licked her lips. 'Daddy, is something wrong? Oh, God! it's not Robert——'

'No, no, no, Sophie!' Doctor Kemble strode towards her, grasping her forearms and shaking her gently. 'Nothing's wrong, so put that out of your head.' He gave her a swift kiss and then looked admiringly at the villa. 'My, my, this is a beautiful place, isn't it? Mrs. Tarrant was not exaggerating.'

'Shall we go inside?' Harriet smiled encouragingly at Sophie, ignoring the questioning look in her eyes. 'It's cooler out of the glare, and I'm sure I can persuade Nana to make us some afternoon tea.'

Sophie led the way into the lounge with its marble-tiled floor and cushion-strewn couches. She linked her fingers tightly together and then said: 'Is—is Mummy with you?'

'No.' Doctor Kemble gestured for permission to sit down and Sophie nodded impatiently. 'No, Sophie, she's at Penn Warren. Simon is back at school, as you know, and someone had to look after him.'

Sophie moved her shoulders helplessly. 'I don't understand, Daddy——'

'You're not looking well, Sophie,' he commented, his fine eyes showing lines of strain. 'Mrs. Tarrant tells me you're not eating.'

Sophie shifted from one foot to the other. 'Why are you here, Daddy?'

'I invited him.' Harriet had entered behind them after issuing the cook with her instructions. 'Won't you sit down, Sophie? Or do you want to go to the bathroom?'

Sophie subsided on to a chair, looking expectantly at the pair of them. 'Please,' she begged. 'There has to be a reason for your coming.'

Harriet nodded. 'There is. Your father has something to say to you.'

'Then what?' Sophie could hardly contain herself.

Doctor Kemble leaned towards her, his hands hanging loosely between his knees. 'I've come—I've come to say that—maybe we were wrong, your stepmother and I. Maybe we shouldn't have—forbidden Robert to have anything to do with you.'

Sophie slumped. 'What?'

Her father sighed. 'Sophie, don't make this any harder than it already is. I've—I've admitted we may have been mistaken. It's difficult to know what else to say.'

Sophie jerked upright. 'It's a bit late to say anything, isn't it?'

Doctor Kemble looked at Harriet, and she shook her head. 'It's never too late, Sophie.'

'But it is! You—you know—how Robert feels——'

'I do. But do you?'

Sophie caught her breath. 'What does that mean?'

'Sophie,' her father was speaking again now. 'Sophie, after you—after you left England, Robert asked to see you.'

'What?' Sophie stared at him.

'It's true.'

Sophie blinked, trying to absorb what he was saying. 'But—why?'

Doctor Kemble shifted uncomfortably. 'Your stepmother told him that you'd returned to Greece.'

'But why did he want to see me?'

Her father sighed again. 'That's not for me to say.'

'And when—when she told him I'd gone?'

'He assumed—he assumed——'

'He assumed you didn't want to see him again,' put in Harriet shortly.

Sophie gasped, staring disbelievingly at her father. 'And you allowed him to think that?'

'It was easier that way.' Her father mopped his brow with his handkerchief. 'Sophie, you know how your stepmother and I have always felt about you and Robert——'

'Oh, *Daddy*!' Sophie felt physically ill. To imagine Robert's reactions when he had found she had returned to Corfu without making any further attempt to see him filled her with horror. Particularly as no one had apparently seen fit to disabuse him of the reasons behind her behaviour. What must he have gone through? Had he believed she had been revolted by his appearance? 'Oh, Daddy, how could you?'

'Sophie, Robert was in hospital. He was still very weak, morose. Laura was convinced that once he was up and about again, once he had had time to consider——'

Sophie got abruptly to her feet and walked away from him. 'So why have you come here?' she demanded unsteadily. 'To clear yourself in case any of this comes out later?'

Her father looked defeated as she turned to face him. 'No, Sophie,' he replied heavily. 'Not for those reasons. I came because Mrs. Tarrant came to Penn Warren and told Robert the truth, and he was in no fit state to make this journey alone.'

'*What?*' Sophie couldn't breathe. Her throat was choked. She stared incredulously at her father and then turned to Harriet. 'You—you mean—Robert's here? In Corfu? At the villa?'

'No, Sophie,' Harriet spoke now, 'not at the villa. He drew the line at that. He's down in the town, at the hotel where he's booked a room. If you want to see him, you have to go to him.'

'If—I—want—to—see—him!' Tears began to overflow Sophie's eyes and stream unheeded down her cheeks. 'Oh, God, of course I want to see him!'

'I told him that,' observed Harriet calmly, 'but I'm afraid he's still a little self-conscious about his appearance——'

'Take me there!' Sophie left her father in no doubt as to the strength of her feelings. 'Oh, please, take me now!'

Doctor Kemble would have got to his feet then, but Harriet stayed him. 'I'll take her,' she stated firmly. 'Then I'll come back and we'll have some tea.'

The drive from the villa down the tortuous slopes to Corfu town had never seemed longer or more uninteresting. Sophie was tense with emotions too long denied and Harriet had more sense than to try and talk to her. However, when she stopped in the square before the hotel, Sophie turned to her and grasped her hand.

'Thank you,' she said tearfully. 'I don't know how, but I must repay you.'

'Just be happy, my dear,' said Harriet gently, her own eyes slightly moist. 'And remember, your parents do love you, no matter how hard to believe that might seem.'

Sophie nodded, impulsively kissed her cheek, and slipped out of the car.

If the hotel receptionist thought there was something rather odd about a young woman who had obviously recently been weeping asking for the room number of one of his guests, he hid it admirably. Perhaps he imagined they were a married couple who had split up after a row, thought Sophie lightheadedly, as she walked along the corridor of the second floor to Robert's room. Perhaps he was more accurate than he knew...

She knocked at Robert's door. She hadn't the courage to turn the handle and walk right in. It was some minutes before the door was answered, and one look at Robert's strained and tired face told her why. He had obviously been resting, and had shed his clothes for the coolness of a shower. His tousled hair was still damp, and a towel was hitched about his hips. The stitches had been removed from his cheek, and now only the savage scars remained.

'Hello, Robert,' she greeted him awkwardly. 'I—I— have I disturbed you?'

Robert stared at her as though he couldn't take his eyes from her. Silently he stood aside, and she entered the functional hotel bedroom. There were no carpets on the rubber-tiled floor, only a plain bedstead covered with a patterned spread, an old-fashioned dressing table and wardrobe, and glass sliding doors which opened on to a wrought iron faced balcony. Robert's clothes were strewn all over the bed, and a suitcase was half open on the floor. Sophie took in all these things in those first few second, her faculties sensitised by an acute awareness of him behind her.

Then she turned. He was standing by the door which he had closed, and she sensed he was as tense as she was. 'How—how are you, Robert?' she asked tremulously.

'I'm much better, thanks,' he replied evenly, touching his scarred cheek with a probing hand. 'As you can see, it's still quite a mess.'

'It's not important. So long as you're all right.' Sophie dismissed the question in his voice.

'How about you? You're looking—pale. I expected you to look fit and healthy.'

Sophie glanced down at her toes. 'Oh, I'm all right. I—er—I've been working . . .'

'Have you?' He hitched the towel more firmly about his lean hips. 'I go to Canada to work in six weeks.'

Sophie shifted from one foot to the other. 'So they didn't sack you?'

'No.'

They might have been strangers exchanging news. Sophie clasped her hands together. 'My—my father said—you wanted to see me.'

'Yes.' Robert raked a hand through his hair.

Sophie moved restlessly. 'Well, I'm here.'

'I know it.' Still Robert made no move towards her. He drew a deep breath. 'I wanted to tell you about Emma.'

'There's no need——'

'Yes, there is.' Robert's voice had hardened slightly. 'I believe she'd told you we were living together—in London?' Sophie nodded and he shook his head. 'It wasn't true. She shared a flat with two other girls.'

'It doesn't matter——'

'It does.' Robert clenched his fists. 'I also have to tell

you that we never slept together.' His mouth twisted as Sophie caught her breath and half turned away. 'Oh— she wanted me to. But I knew I wouldn't have been the first, and certainly wouldn't be the last. I didn't love her—all I could think of was you. So I knew she couldn't be pregnant by me—and yet you immediately believed her story. That was what hurt and disillusioned me.'

'But she said——'

'I can imagine what she said. She thought if she could cause a rift big enough between us, I'd go back to her.'

'Between—us?'

'Oh, *God*! Of course, between us,' he groaned, and reaching for her hauled her into his arms. 'I don't know whether this is why you're here,' he muttered burying his face in the scented hollow of her throat, 'but by God, I can't hold out much longer, Sophie . . .'

Sophie shivered as she slid her arms around his smooth waist. His body was firm and slightly moist, and she yielded against him completely. 'I thought you'd never get round to it,' she whispered provocatively, against his mouth.

He drew her down on to the bed. The towel slipped away, and there was nothing between her and his hard, demanding flesh. It was wonderful after all the days and weeks of pain and humiliation to feel his weight bearing her down, his mouth exploring every inch of her face, seeking the hollow between her breasts, caressing her with conscious possession.

But at last he pushed her away and lay flat on his back, his arms behind his head, just looking at her with lazy abandon. 'Oh, Sophie,' he murmured, half amused, half self-derisory, 'look what you do to me!'

Sophie leant on her elbows beside him, stroking the muscular lines of his stomach. 'So what are you going to do about it?'

His eyes darkened. 'What do you want me to do about it?' He turned towards her. 'Could you bear to see my face when you wake up every morning of your life? Or should I allow you to go to university like your father hoped you would, and have plastic surgery in your absence?'

Sophie flung herself upon him. 'You—you wouldn't force that upon me, would you?'

He half smiled. 'Sophie, all I want is you. I love you.'

'But you sent me away when I came to see you in hospital,' she reminded him softly, her lips caressing his scarred cheek.

He turned his mouth to hers. 'Don't remind me!' He sighed. 'Sophie, that night in your bedroom when your father exploded his bombshell and you believed him, I—I nearly went off my head. Then—when I came back that following weekend and found you prepared to leave for Corfu, I just wanted to escape.'

'From life?' she asked, unsteadily.

'Oh, yes.' He shook his head. 'I admit, the accident was my fault. It wasn't until afterwards I realised how selfish killing myself would have been. Then, when you came to see me, when you told me that you'd marry me whatever Emma's condition—I felt angry, furiously angry. I wanted to ask you why you couldn't have said that in the first place, given me a chance to explain...' He paused. 'But after you'd gone that evening, I began remembering how convincing the parents could be. I recalled how I had behaved when you came home from school. That was why I asked to see you again. When I found you had come back here, I lost all hope.'

'Oh, Robert!' She buried her face in his neck. 'And now?'

'Now?' He lifted her up to look at him. 'Now I'm here——'

'Thanks to Mrs. Tarrant.'

'Yes, thanks to Mrs. Tarrant.'

Sophie frowned. 'What did she tell you about me?'

Robert smiled then. 'Wouldn't you like to know!'

'Tell me!'

He studied her appealing face. 'Well, she said you were fading away for love of me!' His tone was light, but his eyes were solemn. 'Was that the truth?'

'Don't you know?'

His smile widened. 'Oh, yes, I think I do now.'

'Can I come to Canada with you?'

'If you'll marry me first.'

Sophie nodded eagerly, then she sighed. 'Your mother—she might not approve even now. She wanted you to marry Emma.'

'Emma went out of favour weeks ago, as I'm sure you know.' Robert rolled over, imprisoning her beneath him again. 'She'll get used to it. The months we have to spend in Canada will give her time to adapt. And we could always make her a grandmother, which would give her something else to think about . . .'

November paperbacks

FOR THE LOVE OF SARA
by Anne Mather
Joel would never forgive Rachel for the fact that she was going to marry his father!

COLLISION COURSE
by Jane Donnelly
Everyone in the village was thrilled about the arrival of Luke Hannay—everyone except Rosemary Smith!

CORPORATION BOSS
by Joyce Dingwell
Why wasn't Anthony Vine interested in Constance any longer? What had she done?

COBWEB MORNING
by Betty Neels
Alexandra was in love with Taro van Dresselhuys—but so was pretty little Penny . . .

BLADON'S ROCK
by Pamela Kent
Would Richard ever look away from Roxanne and notice Valentine?

ESCAPE TO HAPPINESS
by Mary Whistler
Why should that Society wedding ever intrude into Rose's life? But it did.

PRINCE FOR SALE
by Rachel Lindsay
Melissa married Prince Louis for reasons of state. But she knew he really loved another woman . . .

CROWN OF WILLOW
by Elizabeth Ashton
Could Halcyon stand by and see the man she loved marry for money?

THAT MAN BRYCE
by Mary Wibberley
Who *was* the mysterious Bryce? And how could Kim get away from him?

THE BEACH OF SWEET RETURNS
by Margery Hilton
A glamorous story, set in Malaya, of a girl who never wanted to fall in love again . . .

30p net each
Available November 1975

Also available in November —
Four titles in our 1975 Christmas Pack

THE DEVIL'S DARLING
by *Violet Winspear*

'But you don't know me—you don't love me,' Persepha protested when the magnetic Don Diablo Ezreldo Ruy announced his intention of marrying her. 'In Mexico, *señorita*, the knowing and the loving come after marriage,' he told her. But would they?

COME THE VINTAGE
by *Anne Mather*

Ryan's father had left her a half share of his prosperous vine-growing business, and the other half to a man she had never heard of, a Frenchman named Alain de Beaunes—on condition that they married each other. So, for the sake of the business, they married, neither caring anything for the other. Where did they go from there?

FLAME OF FATE
by *Anne Hampson*

It was years since Alana had seen Conon Mavilis, although she knew he still hated her for having turned him down. Now, in Greece, they had met again, and Conon, smouldering and embittered, was insisting that she become his wife. And this time he had the power to make her agree ...

DARK INTRUDER
by *Nerina Hilliard*

Young Kerry Derwin didn't want this film unit intruding into her peaceful, happy life and turning it upside down. And she wasn't interested in the star, Paul Devron, either. Certainly she wasn't going to add herself to his long list of conquests. But then Kerry hadn't yet actually met Paul Devron ...

£1.20 per pack

Your Mills & Boon Selection!

Over the page we have listed a number of titles which we feel you may have missed or had difficulty in obtaining from your local bookshop over the past months. If you can see some titles you would like to add to your Mills & Boon collection, just tick your selection, fill in the coupon below and send the whole page to us with your remittance including postage and packing. We will despatch your order to you by return!

If you would like a complete list of all the Mills & Boon romances which are currently available either from your local bookshop or, if in difficulty, direct from Mills & Boon Reader Service, together with details of all the forthcoming publications and special offers, why not fill in the coupon below and you will receive, by return and post free, your own copy of the Mills & Boon catalogue—'Happy Reading.'

Why not send for your copy today?

MILLS & BOON READER SERVICE, P.O. BOX 236, 14 Sanderstead Road, South Croydon, Surrey CR2 0YG, England.

Please send me the titles ticked ☐

Please send me the free Mills & Boon Magazine ☐

I enclose £................................(No. C.O.D.) Please add 5p per book—standard charge of 25p per order when you order five or more paperbacks. (15p per paperback if you live outside the UK and Europe).

Name... Miss/Mrs

Address ....

City/Town ....

County/Country................................Postal/Zip Code................

Your Mills & Boon Selection!

☐ 173ᶠ
THE TIMBER MAN
Joyce Dingwell

☐ 243ᶠ
ACCOMPANIED BY HIS WIFE
Mary Burchell

☐ 459
A CURE WITH KINDNESS
Ruth Clemence

☐ 604
**WINDY NIGHT, RAINY
MORROW**
Ivy Ferrari

☐ 640
MUSIC OF THE HEART
Mary Burchell

☐ 658
NOT WANTED ON VOYAGE
Kay Thorpe

☐ 665
IF LOVE BE LOVE
Flora Kidd

☐ 671
BELOVED RAKE
Anne Hampson

☐ 679
THE PENGELLY JADE
Lucy Gillen

☐ 688
HAPPY WITH EITHER
Ruth Clemence

☐ 702
FLUTTER OF WHITE WINGS
Elizabeth Ashton

☐ 708
DEAR ADVERSARY
Kathryn Blair

☐ 719
**THE HOUSE CALLED
GREEN BAYS**
Jan Andersen

☐ 736
A MAN LIKE DAINTREE
Margaret Way

☐ 741
A QUESTION OF MARRIAGE
Rachel Lindsay

☐ 748
THE FROST AND THE FIRE
Gloria Bevan

☐ 752
NOONFIRE
Margaret Way

☐ 757
THE ONE AND ONLY
Doris E. Smith

☐ 762
GENTLE TYRANT
Lucy Gillen

☐ 767
THE SOPHISTICATED URCHIN
Rosalie Henaghan

☐ 776
A TOUCH OF MAGIC
Essie Summers

☐ 782
AFTER SUNDOWN
Anne Hampson

☐ 788
MATAI VALLEY MAGIC
Mary Moore

☐ 793
SPIRIT OF THE SUN
Dorothy Cork

☐ 798
ERRANT BRIDE
Elizabeth Ashton

☐ 803
MAN IN CHARGE
Lilian Peake

☐ 807ᴀ
ROMAN SUMMER
Jane Arbor

**All priced at 20p. Please tick your requirements and use the
handy order form overleaf.**